THE AVENGER

A Walt Slade Western

Bradford Scott

CHIVERS

British Library Cataloguing in Publication Data available

This Large Print edition published by AudioGO Ltd, Bath, 2013.
Published by arrangement with Golden West Literary Agency

U.K. Hardcover   ISBN   978 1 4713 1710 1
U.K. Softcover   ISBN   978 1 4713 1711 8

Printed and bound in Great Britain by
TJ International Limited

THE AVENGER

ONE

Ranger Walt Slade, who the Mexican *peons* of the Rio Grande villages named El Halcon — The Hawk — sang softly to himself as he rode through the starshot dark in the shadow of lonely San Cajo Mountain.

More than six feet in height, wide of shoulder, lean of waist and hip, Slade sat his magnificent horse, Shadow, with the careless grace of a lifetime in the saddle. His lean, hawk-nosed face was marked by long, black-lashed, laughing gray eyes and a rather wide mouth, grin-quirked at the corners. That humorous mouth somewhat relieved the tinge of fierceness evinced by the prominent, high-bridged nose and the square powerful jaw, just as the gay, reckless eyes lent a touch of gaiety to a countenance otherwise stern.

Slade wore the unpretentious garb of the rangeland — faded overalls, batwing chaps, soft blue shirt with a vivid handkerchief looped about his sinewy throat, broad-brimmed "J.B." and well-scuffed, high-heeled half-boots of softly tanned leather. Double cartridge belts encircled his lean waist and from their carefully worked and oiled cut-out holsters protruded the plain black butts of heavy guns from which his slim, muscular hands never seemed far away.

"Shadow," he told the black horse, "Reckon it doesn't want more than a couple of hours till daylight. Then maybe we can locate some place where we can put on the nosebag. I'm gaunt as a gutted sparrow and you're beginning to sink in at the middle as if you'd been squeezed between two gate posts."

Shadow snorted emphatic agreement. Slade chuckled and scanned the eastern sky. Abruptly his eyes narrowed a trifle.

"Say, feller," he exclaimed, "that isn't the sun rising over there, is it? Well, if it is, it's sure trailing its rope off the nighttime reservation. Way too far to the north."

As he gazed, the reddish glow in the northeast grew stronger and widened out. Undoubtedly there was something burning not far off and to all appearances very close to the trail. As Slade puzzled over what it could be, there suddenly sounded loud in the silent night a stutter of gunshots, the spiteful cracks of six-guns punctuated by a deep and sullen boom.

Slade tightened his grip on the reins and settled his feet in the stirrups. "Get going, feller," he told the black horse. "Something's busted loose up ahead and I guess we'd better take a look."

Shadow lengthened his stride. His long legs shot backward like steel pistons, he tossed his shapely head, slugged it above the bit and seemed to literally pour his powerful body over the ground. His gait was a smooth run that ate up the distance. Slade swayed easily in the saddle, balancing the speeding horse with his weight, his hand light on the bridle but guiding his mount with the master touch that imbues a horse with confidence. Watchful, alert, Slade scanned the trail ahead, which wound snakily through thick growth.

Abruptly the trail straightened out, the growth fell back to reveal a wide clearing. Slade let the reins fall on Shadow's neck, his hands dropped to the butts of his guns.

Over to one side, on the west of the trail that now ran almost due north, a building, evidently a barn, was blazing fiercely. Nearer the trail was a well-built cabin, from the dark window of which came a spurt of fire and the dull boom of a heavy rifle.

Fronting the cabin were scattered boulders and clumps of low growth; and behind the boulders and the brush crouched half a dozen men who fired at the cabin window. Slade's swift, encompassing glance showed him that they wore black masks pierced with eye-holes; their hatbrims were pulled low, so that little more than the glint of eyes could be seen.

The men whirled with shouts of alarm as the great black horse crashed around the bend. There was a crackle of shots and bullets whined past horse and rider.

Slade's voice rang out, "Hold it, Shadow!"

The horse skated to a halt, there was a blurring gleam of metal and Slade's big sixes let go. The masked men dived this way and that to escape the hail of lead. One screamed shrilly and pawed at a blood-spurting shoulder. Another reeled back, a scarlet flood staining his black mask. A third pitched forward to lie in a motionless huddle. With yells and curses the others fled wildly toward the fringe of thick brush west of the clearing, leaping and zigzagging. The two wounded men reeled and staggered after the rest.

The rifle inside the cabin boomed sullenly. Slade sheathed his empty Colts with a flicker of movement and slid his heavy

Winchester from where it snugged in the saddle boot beneath his left thigh. But before he could line the long gun the last of the fugitives had vanished into the growth. He heard the crashing of their progress through the brush, a moment of silence, then the beat of fast hoofs fading swiftly into the distance.

For minutes El Halcon sat motionless, listening intently, his eyes searching the growth, rifle at the ready. But the beat of hoofs dimmed to silence. There was no movement amid the chaparral, no sign that the roaring activity of a moment before had been other than an hallucination of the night, save the huddled form lying motionless in the light of the blazing barn.

Slade sheathed the rifle, drew his Colts and replaced the spent shells with fresh cartridges. The cabin window remained dark and he could hear no sound inside the building. He wondered if the defender or defenders had been killed. Perhaps, though, whoever had crouched by the window might be a bit leery of showing himself, which under the circumstances was not surprising. Slade raised his voice in a reassuring shout.

"Okay in there?" he called. "Reckon it's safe to come out now."

There was another moment of silence,

then the door creaked open and an old Mexican stepped into view, a Sharps buffalo gun ready in his hands. Slade chuckled as he glimpsed the ancient and ponderous weapon.

"Figured at first you must have a cannon mounted in there, judging from the racket," he told the old man.

The Mexican smiled, his wrinkled face lighting pleasantly.

"You come at a good time, *Señor*," he replied courteously, speaking in the precise English of the mission-taught Mexican. "The bullets that passed through the window were uncomfortably close, and I doubt not that sooner or later one would have found its mark."

Walt Slade holstered his guns and then swung lithely to the ground. He smiled down at the old man from his great height.

"What was the shindig about?" he asked. "Those masked gents sure didn't stop to ask questions, but started slinging lead at me the minute I rode around the bend. I felt sort of called on to sling a little back. What was it all about?"

The Mexican answered indirectly, his gaze fixed on the huddled form half behind a boulder. *"Señor,"* he said, "you have this night done me a great service, but I fear you have made bad and dangerous enemies. Those men were of the Dawn Riders. I would urge that you ride from here, swiftly and far."

The color of The Hawk's black-lashed eyes seemed to subtly change until they were the gray of the cold mists swathing San Cajo's lofty crest.

"And just who are the Dawn Riders?" he asked.

"Come into the *casa, Señor,*" the Mexican replied. "The home of Sancho Rojas is humble, but he can offer you food and steaming coffee, which is warming to the blood and strengthening to the heart at such an hour as this. The *caballo* you can place in the shed behind the house, where there is ample provender for him."

"Fine, Sancho!" Slade applauded. "We can both stand a bite about now, but —" He glanced questioningly at the fiercely burning barn.

Sancho Rojas shrugged with Latin expressiveness. "It is empty," he replied, "and the building itself cannot be saved. The wind blows from the house so we need not fear the brands. It is ever their way, *Señor.* They fire an outbuilding and when those in the house rush out to quench the flames they shoot them down. It has happened several times. Being familiar with their methods, I did not rush out. I remained inside with my old *escopeta*. I wounded one, I think. I hope it was in the belly and that he will die sweating, with the vultures picking at his eyes!"

"Can't say as I blame you," Slade replied. He supplied his name and they shook hands, the old Mexican favoring him with a searching glance and smiling a little as he pronounced the name. Slade, who did not overlook the slightest details, noted that when next Sancho addressed him, he used the Mexican term of respect, *Capitan*, instead of the impersonal *Señor.*

Slade saw to it that all Shadow's wants were cared for, then he joined Sancho in the cabin. The Mexican at once bolted the heavy door and shuttered and barred the window. Then he busied himself at the stove. Soon the pair sat down to an appetizing meal washed down with many cups of steaming coffee. After they had finished eating, Slade rolled a cigarette, cowboy fashion, with the slim fingers of his left hand, and through the blue film of smoke regarded his host.

"And just who are the Dawn Riders?" he repeated his former question. Sancho shrugged and threw out his hands in a significant gesture.

"*Quien sabe* — who knows — ?" he replied. "There are those who say they are the spirits of the old *bandidos* who lived and died in this dark land. But most think, rightly, I believe, that they are evil men who hide in the mountains and sally forth to raid and slay. Over a year ago they made their first appearance. They drive off cattle from the ranches. They robbed the stage that travels by way of this trail beside which my cabin sits. Once it was a bank in the town of Sanders to the north. Twice they have ridden up to ranchhouses where they knew money was stored, money but recently received for the sale of cattle. Both times, as tonight, they set fire to a building as a means of gaining entrance. Each time they robbed and killed. Always they go masked, and to see the face of one is to die."

"Reckon I'll risk it soon as daylight comes," Slade answered grimly. "I figure to give that sidewinder out there on the ground a once-over."

"I would advise against it, *Capitan*," Sancho replied with emphasis, "it is as if one looked into the Evil Eye."

"The Evil Eye can't hurt you if your heart is clean," Slade replied quietly.

"*Si,* that is so," the Mexican agreed, "and because of that doubtless you will come to no harm."

"Thank you," Slade smiled. "Does anybody know where these bandits hang out?"

Old Sancho shook his grizzled head. "Many are the places in which they might hide," he said. "This is a land accurst, this land between the Nueces and the Great River, the Rio Grande. It is a land of many strange tales — tales of hidden treasure, of blood and violence, of deeds that make one shudder in the hearing. On San Cajo Mountain, in the shadow of which my cabin sits, is a hidden cave wherein much treasure is stored — heaps of bullion, Spanish doubloons, golden candlesticks, bridle bits and spurs of precious workmanship, plated firearms and all manner of other valuable plunder taken from grandees and cathedrals. It was placed there in the old days by *bandidos* who lived in the great cave and preyed on traffic over this, the lower trail between Laredo and San Antonio, or so the story goes. Under the dark waters of the little bay to the south are fragments of ships sailed by men who robbed and murdered but did not live to enjoy their ill gotten gains. There are many stories of buried gold watched by the spirits of those who paid for the blood-drenched treasure with the substance of their souls — gold it is death to seek."

"Mostly stories, I'd say," Slade remarked.

"Yes, stories, for the most part," Sancho replied. The way he said it caused Slade to shoot him a quick glance.

"Ever hear of anything of the kind that wasn't altogether — a story?" he asked.

The old Mexican was silent for a moment, staring at the crack between the closed shutters, which was graying with the approach of dawn. Suddenly, however, he turned his dark eyes upon his guest. He smiled, almost apologetically, and was instantly serious again.

"*Capitan,*" he said, "if you care to listen, there is a story I can tell you that is true. Only I hesitate to tell it, for I truly believe that to hear it and let others know you have heard it is to court death."

"Now just what do you mean by that?" Slade asked.

Again Sancho hesitated, then replied, "Only once have I told the story, to an *amigo* in Sanders to the north, about a year ago. Perhaps the wine we drank together opened my lips. That very night of the telling my friend was slain, none knew by whom. He was found dead in the morning with a knife in his back. And, ridiculous though it may seem, I feel that because I told the story to my friend, who doubtless repeated it when the wrong ears were listening, that tonight the Dawn Riders sought to slay me. Perhaps they believed that I found the treasure and have it stored in my cabin."

"Could be," Slade admitted, "but let's have the yarn. I'll take a chance on getting killed because I heard it, and, if it will make you feel better, I'll promise not to repeat it."

Old Sancho shook his head dubiously, then he chuckled. "As I said before, the Dawn Riders will have marked you for death, so I don't believe hearing the story will make matters worse," he said. "Yes, I will tell you the story. Part of it is well-known, and a very interesting part, but there are other parts known to me alone, for I alone of all men now living in the world was present at the time."

Rolling a cigarette and lighting it, he began to talk, and the old man was an excellent storyteller. Slade felt as if he was a spectator viewing the grim happenings. His lively imagination made it all very real indeed.

Two

The wind blowing across the blue waters of the Gulf was freshening. The sky above was taking on a brassy tint and already the crests of the shoreward surging waves were flecked with white. The sun, which an hour before had been a shimmering golden disc, was subtly changing to a ball of glowing copper edged by an angry aura of purplish flame. From the bar that paralleled the inner shore line came a low moaning as if some sea monster were restless with pain. The salt grass on the sandy flat whispered and rustled, telling the wind secrets of days long gone when the white sails of pirate ships stood out against the skyline as they fled from the thundering guns of the towering Spaniard that rolled in pursuit.

To the east flowed the sinister Nueces, "the deadline for sheriffs," with its grim canyon and its "haunted" parallel lakes. To the northwest San Cajo Mountain loomed mistily dim through the haze, grown with prickly pear and Spanish dagger.

On the sand flat two men toiled in the red rays of the low lying Texas sun. The Harvey brothers, Sid and Blake, long, bony men with quiet eyes, skin tanned to a leathery hue by much outdoor living, and slow, methodical movements, shoveled aside the sand that spewed up from the deep hole with monotonous regularity. From time to time they paused to scan the thickets that bordered the sand flat.

The hole in the sand was nearly four feet in diameter and at the moment so deep that Dirk Pacer, the digger in the depths, and a young Mexican, little more than a boy, who assisted him, were clean out of sight, their presence testified to only by the clicking of a pick and the intermittent flash of Pacer's spade as he threw out the sand for his fellow workers to shove aside.

Suddenly Pacer and the Mexican boy began to cough. The Harveys could hear them retching and gasping. Sid leaned over and peered into the hole. "What's the matter, Dirk?" he asked.

"C-can't breathe! Something seems to be choking me. We're coming up," Pacer replied.

A moment later he came clambering up the short, makeshift ladder. He floundered over the edge of the hole, the Mexican boy close at his heels, and for a few moments lay on the sand breathing in great gulps. The Mexican boy was in a little better shape, but not much.

Finally Pacer got painfully to his feet and wiped the sweat from his face with a sinewy hand that shook a trifle. He was a lean, lanky but broad-shouldered man somewhat older than the Harvey brothers, who were twenty-four and twenty-six respectively, Sid being the older. He was quick and nervous in his movements, with a nervousness that amounted almost to jerkiness. Like the Harveys he wore regulation cow-country garb, and like them he had a heavy gun sagging from his cartridge belt.

"Smells awful down there," he said to his concerned companions.

"Like an open grave that has remained open too long," added the young Mexican.

Big Sid voiced an indulgent chuckle. "You got too much imagination, son," he said kindly. "Likely it's just rotten seaweed washed up when the tide is extra high."

"Could be," Pacer conceded. The Mexican boy did not look convinced and furtively crossed himself.

"Anyhow, I ain't going down again till it has a chance to air out," said Pacer.

"I'll take over for a spell," suggested Blake Harvey.

"Aw, let's knock off for today," said Pacer. "It's getting late and it looks like we're in for a bad night. I think it would be a good notion to fix up that lean-to a bit. We'll need it if it comes on to storm like it looks it will."

Sid Harvey nodded, glancing toward the heavy clouds that were piling up in the south.

"Yep, be dark mighty soon," he agreed. "I ain't over set myself on sticking around here on the flat when the light gets bad. Never can tell who might be holed up in one of them thickets. Somebody might have kept an eye on us when we rode down here, or got a sight of us digging."

"Uh-huh, no sense of taking chances," Pacer concurred heartily.

"Didn't hit anything promising yet?" asked Blake Harvey.

Pacer shook his head. "Nothing but sand and more sand," he grunted. "And that dang hole is getting mighty deep. You're sure for certain we're in the right place, Sid?"

The elder Harvey drew a wrinkled sheet, yellowed and crackling, from an inner pocket and peered closely at the lines and figures traced on it. The cowmen didn't know it, but the sheet was not paper but parchment and undoubtedly very old. Where several lines intersected there was written in the tiny, crabbed lettering of another day, *"My Treasure."*

Neither the Harveys nor Pacer realized that such a notation was highly unusual to such a document. To them it obviously meant that at the spot where the lines crossed the old pirate captain had buried his stolen gold. What else could it mean?

The Nueces country was full of legends, strange yarns, and "maps" that marked the spot where treasure was hidden. Usually they meant nothing, but now and then one had proven to have real significance. Treasure had been discovered, though rarely, so anybody who got hold of some old paper that appeared authentic was convinced that what he had was the real thing. Such was the case with Dirk Pacer and the Harvey brothers. As a consequence they were filled with enthusiasm and hopefully expectant.

Harvey raised his steady eyes and surveyed the landscape. "This is it, all right, if the map is okay, and I believe it is," he said. "I took the sights very carefully and checked and double-checked them. Reckon we just haven't got down deep enough, if there's really anything there."

"Oh, it's there right enough," put in the more optimistic younger brother. "All we got to do is keep digging."

"Well, let's head for camp and get an early start in the morning," urged Pacer. "I can stand a hefty surrounding of chuck and some hot coffee right now, the way I feel. Should help to get that blasted stink out of my nose."

"Okay," agreed Harvey. "That darn wind is blowing harder by the minute. Hope it don't kick the water clean up here when the tide is high. If it does, we'll have all our work to do over. Let's go. Sancho, you get the fire going and rustle something to eat while we tighten up the lean-to a bit."

The Mexican boy nodded and hurried on ahead. He was a likeable young fellow they had picked up on their way down from their ranches farther to the north, not far from San Cajo Mountain. They had hired him to help with the chores.

The others followed at a more sedate pace to a thicket a few hundred paces distant where they had built a rough but service-able shelter in the middle of a thorny patch of *granjano* and black chaparral. The growth was so dense that it in itself provided a good windbreak besides effectually concealing the treasue hunters from possible prying eyes.

Pacer and the Harvey brothers went to work on the lean-to, while Sancho cooked supper. When the meal was ready they ate mostly in silence and with enjoyment.

"Sancho, you sure know how to throw together a surrounding," Sid Harvey said as with a satisfied sigh he drained a final cup of coffee. "You can earn your living cooking anywhere. If we do find the gold and get rich, I've a notion we'll set you up in an eating house business; you'd make a go of it."

The young Mexican smiled with pleasure. He liked these big, kindly men who were always courteous and considerate. He liked Dirk Pacer, too, although that nervous and highstrung individual was more apt to be abrupt and somewhat chary of praise.

After a smoke, the three men stretched out comfortably on their blankets, basking in the heat of the fire, while Sancho cleaned up before seeking his own rest. Sid Harvey again got out the smeary map and studied it.

"Yep, we're right," he remarked. "And, gents, if that old Mexican I got this thing from knew what he was talking about, and I've a mighty strong notion he did, about tomorrow we're due to collect a hefty heap of *pesos*."

"What puzzles me," remarked the more practical Pacer, "is why he didn't go looking for it himself."

"As I told you, old Mexicans like him are a mighty superstitious lot," explained Sid. "Besides, I've a notion he would have come looking for it if he hadn't got cashed in."

Pacer nodded. Sid replaced the map and rolled another cigarette. Outside the wind was howling louder than ever. Ragged

25

masses of cloud drifted across the star-strewn sky. From the bar came the eerie moaning sound, louder than before, rising higher, taking unto itself a shrill note.

"Sounds like somebody bad hurt and not liking it," observed Pacer.

"Maybe it's the old pirate who buried the treasure getting restless because somebody's due to find it," Blake Harvey remarked jocosely.

"Don't gab like that!" growled his elder brother, glancing nervously over his shoulder. "I know it's foolishness, but remember that Mex said bad luck came to everybody who hunted for the stuff. He said haunts cashed 'em in, and he believed it, too. He said the sailor he got the map from said so and told him he got the hurt that finally killed him trying to come back and dig it up. The Mexican was on his way down here to look for it when he got into that cutting that finally did for him. He was dying and knew it when he gave me the map after I tried to do something for him."

"Tarnation, there ain't no such thing as haunts or any kind of ghost!" scoffed Pacer.

"You felt sort of funny down in that hole this evening," Sid Harvey pointed out.

"Uh-huh, but it wasn't no haunts," grunted Pacer.

The Mexican boy, his eyes wide, his lips twitching, surreptitiously crossed himself and muttered an invocation against evil.

"Well, I'll risk 'em in the morning," Blake Harvey said cheerfully. "Right now, gents, I crave a mite of shuteye."

The three rolled up in their blankets. Soon their regular breathing told that the Harvey brothers slept.

The Mexican boy also slept, but fitfully, his mind filled with superstitious terrors.

But Dirk Pacer could not sleep. Perhaps it was the excitement of the treasure hunt, perhaps his unexplained experience of the evening. Anyhow he was nervous and wide awake. He twisted and squirmed in his blankets, rolled and smoked another cigarette and gazed enviously at his sleeping companions. He could hear the wind snapping the twigs of the brush, and the surge of the waters on the rocky shore, while the moaning of the bar grew louder.

Pacer got to thinking. He couldn't sleep, that was certain, and the way he felt now, it would be hours before he finally dropped off. Again he wondered what could have caused the foul odor in the hole. Whatever it was it should have cleared by now and it would be safe to work there. Also, it would be cooler at night. If Sid and Blake weren't such sleepyheads they could all do some digging. They had a lantern and the stars were still shining through rifts in the clouds. Then the idea came. Why not slip out there and do a mite of work himself?

The notion seemed more attractive the more he thought of it. Finally, throwing off the blankets he slipped on his boots, belted his gun about his waist — it was second nature to always pack the thing — and stood up, moving softly so as not to disturb his companions. He eased out from under the lean-to, located the lantern and set out for the excavation in the sand.

A quest for hidden treasure does strange things to men. Minds normally frank and open cloud with suspicion. Close friends and proven associates become targets for distrust. The obvious is a cloak to cover subtle machinations. The natural act is freighted with sinister objectives. Any move the least out of the ordinary is fraught with treacherous implications.

So what happened was not so unreasonable.

Pacer was barely away from the camp when Blake Harvey opened his eyes and stared at the vacant bed. He waited several minutes, listening intently, then reached over and shook his brother.

Sid Harvey was instantly wide awake. "What's the matter?" he asked, sitting up.

Blake gestured to the tumbled blankets. "Dirk just snuck out," he told Sid. "He woke me when he got up. He didn't know it and moved mighty quiet and sneaky. Buckled on his gun and give us a good look before he slid out. I heard him get the lantern. Now what do you suppose he's up to?"

Sid Harvey thought a while, seemed to arrive at a conclusion; his mouth tightened grimly.

"Blake," he said, "didn't it strike you as sort of queer the way Dirk acted this evening, down there in the hole? He got to feeling bad almighty sudden. I was down there the spell before he was and I didn't smell anything or feel bad."

"But Sancho said he felt bad and smelled something, too," Blake objected.

"Sancho's plumb full of imagination," retorted Sid. " 'Cause Dirk began coughing he figured he had to cough, too, and when Dirk said he smelled something, Sancho thought he smelled it. As I said before, Mexicans are superstitious and get scared easy at anything they can't understand. Sancho's scared of haunts and such things and when a feller gets in that frame of mind he'll hear things and see things and smell things what ain't. Maybe Dirk wanted to get Sancho out of that hole before, well before he saw something that maybe Dirk saw."

Blake Harvey stared at his brother, and his own mouth tightened. "And you figure maybe Dirk hit something in that hole before he came up?"

Sid Harvey shrugged his heavy shoulders. "I ain't saying, because I don't know, but — could be," he replied, adding meaningly, "A heap of *pesos* make a bigger heap when they ain't split three ways."

Blake, who had an impulsive streak, threw his blankets aside and swore an explosive oath. "Come on," he growled, reaching for his gun. "We'll see about all this."

The two Harveys strode off together, faces grim, eyes watchful.

Sancho, who also had awakened, and had heard what was said, hesitated a moment, then, his curiosity greater than his fears, stole after them, muttering to himself and making the sign of the Cross. At the edge of the thicket he paused, peering and listening. He hesitated to go farther, partly from the sensible realization that he might stop a bullet fired at a movement in the dark, more so because of the possibility, to him probability, that the sinister spirit of the old pirate captain might be hovering about the hole in the sand, standing guard over his blood-drenched treasure.

But in Sancho Rojas curiosity amounted to almost a vice. He just *had* to know what went on down there by the hole in the sand. Summoning all his courage and murmuring an invocation to his patron saint, he went down on his belly and crept forward cautiously but swiftly, silent as a snake and very nearly as invisible.

Meanwhile Dirk Pacer had almost reached the excavation. The night was dark, lighted only by the eerie glow of the stars flickering through the changing rifts in the clouds, and he made slow progress, partly due to the fact that he paused from time to time to scan the thickets and clumps of brush he passed. Although not superstitious like Sancho, Pacer was also an imaginative man and he peopled the dark growth with possible watchers with designs on the buried gold.

For this reason he did not light the lantern but stole along by the feeble glimmer of the occasional stars in the cloudy sky. Finally, however, he reached the excavation, paused a moment to glance keenly around and then groped his way down the short ladder. He placed the lantern on the bottom of the hole and fumbled for a match. Before he located one he paused, wrinkling his nose with distaste. The unpleasant odor was still strong in the hole, plugging his nostrils, irritating his throat. He swore disgustedly under his breath, leaned against the sandy side of the pit and considered what to do.

But as he pondered, the choking sensation in his throat intensified. There seemed to be a band of steel about his chest, constricting it. His heart beat heavily and laboriously, as if a clutching hand was slowly tightening its grip on the organ.

To Pacer's mind came remembrance of the tales of ghostly watchers who guarded the treasure.

"Blasted foolishness!" he scoffed under his breath; but nevertheless he turned rather hurriedly to the ladder. The digging could wait till daylight.

Forgetting the lantern, he mounted the rungs much faster than he had descended them. He gulped a great draught of the keen night air as his head cleared the surface, clambered over the edge of the pit and straightened up.

Gigantic in the gloom, two menacing figures loomed before him. A suddenly appearing star glinted its light on a gun barrel.

Dirk Pacer went for his six. He was noted for his fast gunhand and straight shooting.

The big Colt was spurting flame the instant it cleared leather.

There was a choking yell, then a roar of answering shots.

Dirk Pacer reeled back, blood streaming down his face and gushing from his side. He managed to empty his gun before he fell, his finger still clinched on the trigger.

As if the boom of gunfire had been a signal, the storm that had been gathering broke in elemental fury. Lightning split the black bosom of the cloud bank. A torrent of flame seemed to fall to the earth no great distance away. The boom of the thunder was followed by an awesome rumbling and crashing, as if the very world itself were dissolving into chaos. A swishing torrent of rain pitted the sand and dimpled the dark surface of the little bay around which the flat curved. The wind increased in violence and the crash of the waves against the rocks rivalled the reverberations of the thunder overhead.

Against the rocks and over them! The rising tide, driven by the mighty force of the gale, was swirling and questing up the gentle rise of the flat. Farther and farther it crept, advancing, retreating, advancing again. A thin film of water coiled and lapped about the bodies of the dead men lying beside the dark hole in the sand. It beat against the sand banked at the edge of the hole. Under its persistent gnawing, sand began to trickle into the excavation. More and more fell as the pressure of the encroaching water increased. With a sighing sound, one whole side of the pit caved in. The water hissed in triumph and poured into the depression, bringing down more sand. The forward creeping, monotonously receding tide smoothed and caressed the loose sand, until all traces of the excavation had vanished and the surface of the flat was level as before.

The tide rose a little higher, but it did not rise high enough or grow sufficiently strong to float the bodies out to the sea.

Long before the rising water reached the excavation, right after the shooting, in fact, Sancho Rojas fled in panic-stricken terror. With trembling fingers he got the rig on his horse and rode madly away from the haunted clearing.

THREE

"And now, *Capitan,* comes the part of the story well known to many," Sancho interpolated, smiling at his attentive listener.

Three days after that fatal night on the

34

sand flat, young Arn Harvey awoke to see his brothers' horses, without saddle or bridle, standing patiently by the corral gate.

Arn Harvey realized that something was terribly wrong. The well-trained horses would not have strayed. With a heart beating with apprehension he saddled up and rode furiously to the Booger F, Dirk Pacer's spread, which adjoined the Harveys' Diamond H. He found the ranchhouse locked. He had no way of telling whether Pacer's horse had also returned, for he did not know which horse Pacer had ridden when he and the Harvey brothers set out on their hunt for buried gold.

Arn knew the general direction in which the treasure seekers had headed. Without delay he loaded a pack horse with provisions and set out in search of them.

The twilight of the second day was glooming the thickets and flats when he found the bodies of his brothers sprawled on the sand. Beside them lay their guns. Blake's had been fired twice, Sid's three times. There was no trace of Dirk Pacer.

Standing over the bodies, Arn Harvey reconstructed the tragedy in his own mind. He saw the three men bearing away the treasure of gold they had discovered, saw the look of avarice and greed in Dirk Pacer's black eyes. He saw the swift movement of his hand, heard the roar of gunfire. It was not surprising, he realized, that Pacer had come out on top in the battle, even with the odds against him. He was noted for his skill with a gun, while the Harveys were not good shots. Arn saw Pacer ride away, bearing with him the treasure for which he had murdered his friends.

Young Arn gulped in his throat, knuckled his eyes with a boyish hand, and swore an oath of vengeance.

Arn Harvey was a husky young fellow almost seventeen. His brothers had looked upon him as a kid, but he was a good cowhand and capable of running a spread. He managed to load the bodies onto the pack horse and set out through the night for the ranch.

Arn found the smeary treasure map in Sid's pocket, after he reached the ranch-house. At first he was tempted to destroy the accurst thing, but changed his mind and laid it aside.

Feeling ran high in the section over the killing of the popular Harveys. Posses rode the wild country between the Nueces and the Rio Grande, but found no trace of Dirk Pacer.

It was some time after his brothers' funeral

that Arn Harvey showed the treasure map to the county surveyor. The surveyor scanned it with a technical eye and was interested.

"Three tie points," he told Arn. "San Cajo Mountain is the apex of an isosceles triangle — that's a triangle with two sides the same length. The other points are chimney rocks standing close to the shore of the bay and a thousand yards apart. These lines inside the big triangle bisect the angles. Where they intersect is the spot marked to dig. With this map all a feller would need to do is locate the chimney rocks, and that should be easy. You say there were no signs of digging where you found the bodies?"

Arn Harvey shook his head. "Nary a sign," he replied.

"Arn," the surveyor exclaimed, "I've a notion they hadn't even started to dig. If they had a row over dividing the stuff it would have most likely happened where they took it out of the hole, not after they packed it off. I figure they got into a row over where to dig. Dirk Pacer was a horny sort and mighty quick to get his bristles up, and Blake Harvey would crawl your hump mighty sudden, too."

"But why would Pacer trail his rope after the shooting if that was the way of it and he didn't have anything worth while to pack along?" demanded Arn Harvey.

The surveyor was ready with an explanation. "Your brothers were pretty well-liked in this section," he answered. "You couldn't say the same for Dirk Pacer. He was a bit too quick to go on the prod and had a habit of saying what he thought and not always in a nice way. Folks didn't cotton to Dirk over much. Reckon he figured the safest thing for him to do was trail his rope."

Young Harvey was forced to admit this sounded reasonable.

"Do you figure you could locate the spot where you found the bodies?" the surveyor asked.

Arn was dubious. "I just couldn't say for sure," he admitted. "I'd been following the coast line all day and it was getting dark. I was so busy watching for some sign of the boys I didn't pay much attention to the country."

"Two chimney rocks a thousand yards apart shouldn't be hard to spot," the surveyor mused. "What do you say, Arn, suppose you and I take a little jaunt down in that direction and see what we can find? I'll pack along my compass and Jacob's Staff and we'll take sights and pin that spot right down where it should be according to the map."

"The boys had a compass," Arn Harvey observed. "Sid knew how to work the thing, but I don't."

"Oh, you could do pretty well with a tape, and a forked stick to sight over," the surveyor replied. "But with a compass we can be exact."

Arn Harvey was still dubious, but he agreed to throw in with the surveyor and they set out on their trip of exploration. They followed the coast line for many miles but never could sight the two chimney rocks standing a thousand yards apart. Only once did Arn feel that he was close to the spot where he had found his brothers' bodies.

"But there aren't any two chimney rocks," the surveyor pointed out. "There's one over there, with the water washing against it, but one isn't two. Nope, this can't be it."

Finally they gave up in disgust.

"The dang map's wong, I reckon," said the surveyor.

"Maybe the old Mex Sid got the map from told him things that ain't written down," Arn suggested.

"Could be," admitted the surveyor, "but it appears everybody who knew anything about it has cashed in their chips. Let's head for home."

Dirk Pacer left no heirs that anybody knew about, so it was logical that Arn Harvey should take over the Pacer spread, which adjoined the Diamond H. The section agreed it was the right thing.

Years passed, and Arn Harvey prospered. The older Harvey brothers had held that a cow that couldn't chaw enough water out of prickly pear to get along in the dry weather wasn't worth having, but Arn Harvey had more progressive notions. Numbers of little tin windmills pumped water from the wells he drilled and kept his stock well supplied. He made other improvements, bred carefully, and was shrewd about marketing.

And as his hair whitened he grew more mellow. The story of the treasure quest and the killings became legends told in lonely cow camps or passed on by other seekers of buried gold. Many sought the spot marked by two chimney rocks near the water's edge, but none found it. Arn Harvey never searched again, although he kept the old map, and as time went on felt more lenient toward the almost forgotten Dirk Pacer. After all, his brother Blake had been quick to go on the prod. Pacer might not have been altogether to blame.

And then, nearly forty years after that

night of storm and death, a stranger rode up to the Diamond H ranchhouse. Arn Harvey, now "Old" Arn Harvey, hospitably invited him to, "Light and line your flue with chuck; the dough-wrangler's just bellered."

The stranger, a tall, broad-shouldered man of perhaps thirty or a little more, with a lean, dark face, twinkling black eyes and a ready smile, accepted the invitation. Together he and the ranch owner entered the dining room and sat down, facing one another across the table.

In true cow country fashion, the meal was consumed largely in silence. Finally the stranger shoved back his plate and reached for the makin's. Through the smoke of the cigarette he regarded his host.

"Name's Harvey, Arn Harvey, isn't it?" he stated rather than asked.

"Always sort of had a notion it is," Harvey agreed.

The other took a deep drag on his cigarette, blew out the smoke and stated,

"Mine's Pacer — Miles Pacer."

Arn Harvey started, his gray eyes narrowing a little. "Heard that name — the last part of it — before," he remarked.

The stranger nodded. "Reckon the first part of the one you heard was Dirk, eh?"

Arn Harvey stiffened in his chair. "Relation of yours?" he asked quietly.

Miles Pacer's black eyes smiled at Harvey.

"Dirk Pacer was my dad," he said softly.

Arn Harvey stared. He opened his lips to speak, but Miles Pacer broke in before he could get the words out.

"I know what you're thinking about, Mr. Harvey," he said, "but do you figure it's just fair to hold against me what happened before I was born? I'm not saying that Dad was altogether in the right in that shooting, but from what he told me about it just before he died last year, I've a feeling he was more in the right than folks hereabouts have been thinking. Dad told me, and I believed him, that it was a fair fight. He and your brothers had an argument over where was the right place to dig for that blasted gold. One thing led to another and it ended in a row. Dad was pretty handy with a gun, as perhaps you know. It seemed your brothers weren't so good; but they were good enough to gun him proper before the shindig was over. After the smoke cleared, Dad was unconscious with a bad head wound and a couple of slugs through his body. He laid out in the rain all night. Didn't regain consciousness till after daylight."

Arn Harvey grunted. "Why didn't he

come back here and tell what happened if he wasn't altogether to blame?"

Miles Pacer smiled, his exceedingly disarming smile, and proceeded to explain in a most persuasive manner.

"When Dad come to in the morning, he was still a long ways from being right in the head — he had a hole through the top of it. He got up just enough strength to crawl to where they had made camp for the night. After a while he got the rig on his horse and managed to climb into the hull. He started riding, didn't really know in what direction he was heading. Had some sort of a vague notion he should get back to the ranchhouse and tell what had happened. But pretty soon he felt himself going again. He twisted his spurs in the stirrup straps and sagged down on his horse's neck. Evidently he fell off after a while. When he came to again he was lying on blankets and a couple of Mexicans were doing what they could for him. He was a mighty sick man and almost immediately he became delirious and started gabbing about the gold and the shooting; wouldn't answer questions. Chances are he couldn't even hear them. The Mexicans were heading back to *mañana* land where they worked as *vaqueros* on a big spread down below the Line. They decided the best thing, in fact the only thing, was to pack Dad along with them to where he could get proper care. They did just that. It's a wonder Dad managed to live through the trip, but he did, but weeks passed before he was able to set a foot on the ground. Meanwhile he had done a lot of thinking and decided it was best for him not to go back to Texas. He figured his story would sound mighty funny to folks after all that time, especially when, according to what he told me, your brothers were mighty popular in the section while he wasn't so well liked. So when he got strong enough he took a job of riding for the old *Don* who owned the big spread, figuring that later, when things had cooled down a bit, he'd go back to Texas and give himself up and tell his story."

Arn Harvey nodded thoughtfully; he could understand how Dirk Pacer must have felt. "But he never did come back," he commented.

"That's right," conceded Miles Pacer, "but there was a reason. One of the Mexicans who saved his life had a sister, a mighty nice girl, pure Spanish blood. Dad fell in love with her and married her. A couple of years later I came along. She died before I was big enough to remember much about her and Dad was left alone to take care of me. So he stayed on with old *Don* Alvarez and when I got big enough to fork a hull I went to work for him, too. Last year Dad took sick and knew he was going to take the big jump. So he called me in and told me the whole story and told me about the spread he owned up here. He said that unless it had been sold for taxes, he still owned it and that by right it should belong to me. He gave me this paper. Of course I don't know anything about the holding so I'm leaving everything up to you."

Pacer drew a folded paper from his pocket and passed it to Arn Harvey. The old cowman took it and examined it carefully. It was a rough but accurate sketch of the old Pacer spread, the Booger F, with boundary lines properly marked, the site of the ranchhouse noted and other details jotted down just as it was to be expected Dirk Pacer would have noted them.

Miles Pacer watched him intently as he studied the drawing. He said nothing more. Arn Harvey rasped his big chin with his fingers and for a while sat deep in thought, the sketch still held in his other hand.

Arn Harvey was an eminently fair man. Also he was well off. He did not deny to himself that a sizeable portion of his wealth had come from the Booger F, the use of which he had had for more than thirty years. In addition he liked Miles Pacer's looks and was impressed by his implied willingness to abide by his, Harvey's decision, and accept it without protest.

The final upshot of the matter was that Arn Harvey shook hands with Miles Pacer and turned over the Booger F to him. As little formality accompanied the transaction as there had been when Arn Harvey took charge of the spread after the disappearance of Dirk Pacer so many years before. When the story got around, it was generally conceded that Arn Harvey did the right thing again.

Miles Pacer proved to be a good cattleman and a good neighbor. He did not shirk his responsibilities and was scrupulously fair in all his dealings. Harvey had expected that he would bring up *vaqueros* of his acquaintance from below the Line to work the ranch, but instead he hired local cowboys. He was active against the wideloopers who were plaguing the section and helped with schemes to run down the sinister and mysterious Dawn Riders who began operations in the section shortly before his arrival and right after the big oil strike on the Ray ranch to the east. He was also a frequent visitor of the Diamond H. All in all, Arn

Harvey did not regret his generous act.

One day Harvey showed Pacer the old treasure map, as he had a habit of doing with visitors, and they chuckled over it together. Immediately, however, Pacer grew serious.

"Those danged things have been responsible for untold trouble," he said bitterly. "And almost always they don't mean a thing."

"Well, this one won't cause any more trouble," Harvey replied cheerfully. "It sure ain't worth nothin', and the only person who knows just where that place is is very likely dead. I mean the Mexican boy — I never knew his name — who went down there with Sid and Blake and your dad. He evidently got away alive, but the chances are he got such a scare he never went back. Mexicans are superstitious and I reckon he'd figure ghosts and things were watching over the place. Yep, he'd be an old man now if he's still alive."

"Very likely he's dead," Pacer agreed disinterestedly, and the subject dropped.

FOUR

His story finished, old Sancho Rojas sat regarding his guest.

"But why didn't you come forward and tell what you knew about what happened?" Slade asked. "You saw that Pacer didn't recognize who was coming toward him from the dark and started shooting, and of course the Harveys shot back."

"Because, *Capitan,* I feared," Sancho explained. "I fled in terror for many miles. Remember, I was but a boy. If I had known that a wounded man lay there on the sands perhaps I would have gone to his aid, but I thought all were dead — they certainly looked it. I did steal back the next day, when the rain had ceased and the sun was bright, and peered from the shelter of the thicket. When I saw that the hole in the sand had vanished and but two bodies lay there I was again stricken with terror. In my ignorance I did not stop to reason that the high tide of that stormy night had washed the loose sand back into the hole and smoothed it over and that the *Señor* Pacer had been but wounded and had recovered enough to ride off. I thought that the spirits who guarded the gold had carried off to hell the body of one of those who sought to rob them of their treasure. Later, after I had attended the school kept by the good *padres* of the mission and had harkened to their teachings, I lost much of my belief in evil spirits. Although," he added with a wry smile, "after what happened to my *amigo* to whom I told the story, added to what happened last night, I am inclined to wonder if the *padres* might not have been wrong and that the spirits who guard the blood-stained gold, if gold there is, are angry at the telling. Perhaps I should not have told you."

Slade chuckled and glanced at his host with merry eyes. "I don't think you believe that at all, Sancho," he replied. "Anyhow, I'll take a chance on the spirits; the only ones I ever knew to make trouble for somebody are the kind that live in a bottle. Do you think you could find that place again, Sancho?"

"Doubtless I could," the Mexican replied. "Perhaps not the exact spot where the hole was dug, but the place in general, yes. But pray do not ask me to guide you there, *Capitan.* If you do, I cannot refuse, but verily I believe the place is accurst. Also I doubt if there is really any gold to be discovered."

"Gold is where you find it, and how you find it," Slade replied cryptically. "And sometimes the form in which it is found is strange indeed."

Slade had indeed found the story engrossing. Aside from being, the way Sancho told it, a vivid portrayal of grim and tragic

49

adventure with a most interesting aftermath, it provided him with some valuable information relative to the section and its inhabitants.

One phase of the yarn in particular intrigued him. Before he joined the Rangers, Walt Slade had graduated from a famous college of engineering. His plan had been to take a post graduate course to round out his technical education, but the loss of his father's ranch because of seasons of blizzard and drought, and the elder Slade's untimely death, had made that for the time impossible. So when Captain Jim McNelty, with whom Slade had worked some during summer vacations, suggested that he sign up with the Rangers for a spell while continuing his studies, Slade had decided it was a good notion. It was a good notion, in a way, too darn good, in fact. He had ample spare time in which to pursue his education and had long ago gotten as much and more than the post grad course could have given him. But there was a catch to the business. Slade had become intensely interested in Ranger work and was loath to sever connections with the famous corps. He still planned to be an engineer some day, but he was young and there was no hurry; he'd stick with the Rangers for a while.

So, due to his educational advantages, Slade analyzed that particular incident of Sancho's yarn with the mind and knowledge of a geologist.

"You say that when you were down in that hole you felt as if you were choking?" he asked.

"Indeed, yes," Sancho replied. "It was as if a bony hand gripped my throat, shutting off my breath. My heart fluttered like a caged bird, my brain swam, there was a bubbly mist before my eyes and in my ears a bell tolled. Little wonder, *Capitan,* that a superstitious boy was terrified. Something did grip my throat. And the smell, it was horrible, like to the stench of decaying flesh. I felt indeed that death was my portion."

"I've a notion you're lucky to be alive, all right," Slade conceded grimly. "You didn't happen to light a cigarette while you were down there?"

"It is doubtful," Sancho replied. "I did not smoke so much in those days and we were very busy."

Slade nodded. Sancho glanced at him expectantly but Slade did not pursue the discussion. Instead his next question appeared to Sancho to be a change of subject.

"The George Ray ranch isn't very far from here, is it?" he asked.

51

"But a few miles to the east," Sancho replied. "That is where they made the great oil strike a year ago. Because of which the town of Sanders to the north has boomed and much evil has come to the section along with great wealth."

"And the sand flat where you dug, how far is that from the Ray holdings?"

"Less than twenty miles to the south," Sancho estimated.

Slade nodded again and stood up. He stretched his long arms above his head, his fingertips almost touching the ceiling. He glanced at the shutters, through which a shaft of brilliant sunshine was streaming.

"Some more coffee?" Sancho suggested.

"That's the best thing you've said yet," Slade smiled. "Then we'll go out and give that punctured gent a once-over."

After drinking the coffee they repaired to the clearing where the body lay.

The slain bandit proved to be a rather nondescript individual, stocky and muscular with dark eyes now glazed in death.

"The kind you pass by in a crowd without a second look," Slade commented. "Folks very seldom do wear their true character on their faces. Let's see what he's got on him; might tie up with somebody or something, though I doubt it."

The man's pockets did not reveal anything of significance. He wore regulation rangeland garb and his gun was an ordinary forty-five. Slipped down over his chin was a black handkerchief cut with eyeholes.

"One of the Dawn Riders without a doubt," said Sancho.

"Perhaps, and then again perhaps not," Slade answered. "Wouldn't be surprised if the Dawn Riders, as you call them, don't wear masks at all. Whenever a trademark of some kind is assigned to a successful owl-hoot bunch, every brush popper who sets up in business tries to emulate them in every way possible. I recall that over around Marathon at the northern edge of the Big Bend country, a few years back, an outfit wearing yellow shirts started operating. Because of the shirts they were called the *Dorados.* They raised plenty of trouble for a while. Well, before you knew it, yellow shirts were spotted near Presidio way down on the Rio Grande and at Sanderson, fifty miles east of Marathon, on the same day. So unless the *Dorados* had managed to set aside the axiom of physics, that nobody can occupy two different spaces at the same time, there was something off-color about the business. I wouldn't be surprised if plenty of black masks will be seen in this section for a while."

"Doubtless you are right," agreed Sancho, adding, "for when was El Halcon ever wrong!"

"So you spotted me, eh?" Slade smiled.

"Of course," Sancho replied. "Who of the humble people of the Border country does not know or has not heard of El Halcon, the friend of the lowly? Now let those who do evil hereabouts beware!"

"I hope you're right," Slade said, his eyes all kindness. "Now we'll pack this gent over in the shade and cover him with a blanket. When I get to Sanders I'll notify the sheriff and he can ride down and look him over. I don't think you have anything to worry about for a while, but I'll keep an eye on you just the same."

He did not feel it necessary to tell the old man that he was much of the opinion that he himself would be the chief recipient of the outlaws' attention.

"My *escopeta* will always be handy and I will not hesitate to use it," Sancho declared cheerfully. "I do not fear."

"Good man!" Slade applauded. "How far is it to Sanders?"

Sancho gestured to the northeast. "Follow the trail and you must arrive there," he said. "It is close to fifteen miles. Some ten miles

54

to the north and east you will pass a large white ranchhouse set in a grove of pinions, which is the *casa* of the *Señor* Arn Harvey of whom I spoke. Five miles farther and you reach the town."

Slade said good-bye to the old Mexican and headed up the trail, singing softly to himself. He was alert and vigilant, as usual, eyes and ears missing nothing, but his thoughts were not altogether on his surroundings.

He was puzzled about the happenings of the night before. He considered the explanation of the attack advanced by Sancho as a bit far-fetched. The fatal treasure hunt had taken place many, many years before. Admitting for the sake of the argument that Sancho had later gone back and dug up the gold, he would certainly have spent it long before now. It was ridiculous to believe that anyone would assume that he still had it cached in his little cabin. Of course a blood feud might be involved, not uncommon to the people south of the Rio Grande, which Sancho didn't consider or had preferred not to mention. That could be the explanation of the attack.

Equally senseless appeared the killing of his friend to whom he had told the story of the hunt and perhaps revealed the location of the sand flat. Slade doubted if there was any tie-up between the two incidents. But there was a bit of coincidence involved that couldn't be altogether ignored. Did somebody want to make sure that neither Sancho nor his friend would visit the spot? If so, why? It appeared that Sancho, and possibly his dead friend, had been the only living persons who knew just where the spot was. If somebody else knew, the mysterious somebody, believing that the gold really existed, would logically have hurried to dig for it. If he didn't know where the place was, why should he desire to eliminate the only persons who did know? The natural procedure would be to try to induce Sancho, by force or otherwise, to guide him there.

Slade found himself right back where he had started. All the available evidence pointed to a desire on the part of somebody to make sure that Sancho should not return to the site of the supposedly buried treasure. Why? Slade didn't have the answer, but somehow he felt that answer was highly important.

"I just got a hunch, that's all," he confessed to Shadow, "but more than once I've found hunches worth following, and I can't help but feel this one will be valuable in cleaning up the mess we were sent here to tackle."

He had covered perhaps half the distance to where Sancho said the Diamond H ranchhouse was located when, on rounding a sharp turn where the trail flanked a precipitous, brush-grown hillside he saw something that will always catch the attention of a horseman riding a narrow trail.

A dozen yards ahead, where the trail began to curve around a thin bristle of thicket, a rattlesnake was coiled, or rather lay in its loose loop in the center of the track.

Slade's hand tightened on the bridle. His other hand dropped to his gun belt. Then his keen glance, which took in all details of an object instantly, noticed something peculiar about the reptile. The rattler's head was raised threateningly, but its tail lay prone in the dust!

El Halcon's mind was as hair-trigger quick as his eyes. His right knee clamped hard against Shadow's ribs.

As if activated by a released spring, the black horse leaped sideways on bunched feet. Slade swayed his body far to the left in unison with his careening mount.

FIVE

Even as Shadow sprang, from the thicket ahead bluish smoke spurted. A bullet screeched through the space Slade's body had occupied the instant before. So close was the whining slug that Slade felt the lethal breath of its passing.

Almost before Shadow landed on his braced legs, Slade's guns were out and streaming fire. Back and forth he raked the thicket ahead with a stream of lead.

The bush was violently agitated. It burst asunder with a crash and a man's body rolled out onto the trail to lie in a huddle on its side, facing the alert Hawk.

Slade's eyes never left the prostrate form. His guns jutted forward, the muzzles rock-steady. The drawn-back hammers were held from falling only by the pressure of his thumbs on the milled tips.

But the body lay without sound or motion, huddled in the dust. Slade could see a widening stain darkening the left shoulder of the man's dirty gray shirt.

El Halcon holstered his guns, swung down from the saddle and took a step forward. In one blinding ripple of motion he hurled himself sideways and down, his gun streaking out as he fell.

Two shots rang out as one. Again Slade felt the wind of a passing bullet. The body in the dust half sprang from the ground, stiffened grotesquely and flopped over on its back, a smoking six falling from a nerveless hand.

For a moment Slade lay with his gun trained on the corpse that had so unexpectedly come to life. But this time the drygulcher was satisfactorily dead, a blue hole between his glazing eyes.

Slade got to his feet, studied the growth ahead and noted that a flock of small birds had just settled into it and were pecking and chirping as they would not have done had the brush concealed a second drygulcher.

"Talk about cold nerve and guts!" Slade remarked to Shadow, apropos of the dead gunman. "With that hole through him and knocked clean from under his hat, he laid there and waited for his chance to put a window in me! He'd have gotten away with it, too, if I hadn't seen the glint of his eyes as he opened them a mite. Well, they didn't wait long to even things up!"

One glance at the dark, sinewy face with its high cheek bones, thin lips, beady black eyes and lank black hair cut in a square bang across the forehead told Slade that the drygulcher was undoubtedly a pure blood Yaqui Indian. He glanced at the dead snake in the trail.

That was an old Yaqui trick, and one that worked more often than it didn't. The drygulcher, perhaps knowing the reputation of the man he planned to waylay or figuring that at least he would be keeping a close watch on everything that went on around him, feared that when Slade rounded the bulge he might spot him. That would have made things uncomfortable even for the drygulcher. So he fixed the dead snake in the trail, knowing that a man seeing a rattler on the prod in his horse's path usually hasn't eyes for anything else.

But he had slipped up on one little detail. He had carefully propped up the snake's head with a thin forked twig but had forgotten to prop up the tail, and an angry rattlesnake always has its tail erect, its rattles buzzing. Overlooking that single detail had caused his attempt to fail and had cost him his life.

Slade gazed down, almost regretfully, at the brave man lying dead in the dust. Many Texans maintained that Yaquis were utterly depraved and vicious, but Walt Slade knew it was not so. It was just that their code of ethics differed from and was sometimes diametrically opposed to that of the white man. The forefathers of the man who lay before him, for countless ages had kept themselves alive by just such stratagems. And centuries of mistreatment and oppression at the hands of the Spanish conquerors and those who came after them gave the Yaqui little reason to love the white man. It was not altogether illogical that he felt justified in employing any means to even up the score.

Slade examined the contents of the man's pockets and found nothing of significance; but the Yaqui's neckerchief instantly caught his attention. It was of heavy black silk of fine quality, with eyeholes cut in the fabric.

Undoubtedly the man had belonged to the outfit that attacked Sancho's cabin the night before. The survivors of the fight, reasoning that the man who frustrated their attempt to kill the Mexican would eventually ride on to Sanders, had laid their ambush accordingly, and with care and patience.

"Nice people!" Slade muttered. "Well, if any of them happen to be hanging around town when the sheriff packs this gent in, it may give them a bit of a jolt."

Browsing around through the growth, he discovered the dead man's horse tethered to a branch. It bore a Mexican brand with which he was unfamiliar and which, he well knew, meant little. He removed the leather from the animal and turned it loose to fend for itself. The rig was plain, well worn and with not even the maker's name stamped on the saddle tree.

With a last glance at the drygulcher and his grisly companion in death, Slade mounted Shadow and rode on toward Sanders, his eyes thoughtful and very watchful. A little later he passed the ranchhouse that he knew must be Arn Harvey's home. Nobody appeared to be about at the moment, however, so he rode on.

The afternoon was plenty well along before Slade sighted Sanders, what had once been a sleepy cowtown but was now a roaring boom town. There were still plenty of weatherbeaten old false-fronts and 'dobes, but on all sides were structures of glaring newness. As he drew nearer the settlement he saw the shimmering twin lines of a railroad crossing the trail he was riding. A moment later a long freight train crashed past with a clang of flashing siderods, the grind of spinning drivers on the rails, the clang and jangle of couplers and brake rigging and the thundering roar of the great locomotive's pounding exhaust. His nostrils stung to the acrid whiff of coal smoke and hot oil, and as the cars rumbled past the air was heavy with the pungent tang of sweating cattle crowded close together in the rocking carriers. Undoubtedly there was plenty of beef shipped from the section. There was money in the section, lots of it, and more coming in with the oil and gas strikes only a few miles distant increasing daily. All of which made for prosperity and well-being; but it also meant increased outlaw activity. No wonder a smart and salty outfit had picked the section for its stamping ground. Different from the old days when a herd of rangy longhorns or an occasional payroll was the best the owlhoots could hope to drop a loop on.

He reached the town, which was indeed a bustling combination of clapboard shacks, unpainted false fronts and substantial buildings boasting much plate glass.

Just the same, Sanders was still a typical shipping town and supply depot for the big ranches of the neighborhood. Saloons, dance halls and gambling establishments were plentiful, rendered more opulent by the stream of gold pouring in from the oil wells nearby. It was safe to say that the population had tripled in the past six months, and the crowds on the streets and packing the various places of recreation were heterogeneous. Cowboys in vividly colored shirts and neckerchiefs tramped the board sidewalks or forked their cayuses in the dust of the unpaved streets. Slade saw Mexican *vaqueros* in black velvet adorned with much silver, barefooted *peons* with dark faces and sad, wistful eyes. Everywhere was a busy, cheerful air reminiscent of San Antonio in its boom days, or Beaumont after the Spindletop gushers began pouring black gold over the prairie.

"She's an up and coming *pueblo,* all right," he told Shadow as he looked for a livery stable where the big black could receive proper treatment.

He located one on a quiet alley and turned Shadow over to a leathery old fellow with frosty eyes and a limp. A crippled cowpoke who had turned to stable keeping at the end of his riding days, Slade surmised.

"You can get fair to middlin' chuck at the Widow Maker right around the next corner," the keeper replied to Slade's question relative to food for himself and a place to sleep. "The whiskey ain't any fuller of snakes than the average and they got rooms for rent upstairs. Nothing fancy but clean and no bugs. The dance floor girls are nice and the games are plumb straight. No gals that roll drunks and no crooked dealers for Border Shift Brewster who runs the joint and does a pretty good job of it. A nice feller, Border Shift. You'll know him by seeing his belly come around the corner thirty seconds before the rest of him hoves into sight. The sheriff's office? Go right on past the Widow Maker half a dozen doors and you can't miss it. Sheriff's name is Bascomb, Ezra Bascomb, and he's all right. Mind's sort of slow, I figure, but his gun hand ain't. But like lots of slow thinking fellers he usually figures things out right after a while. Liable to be a bit crusty but don't mind that. He's got his hands full with trouble of late and it makes him a mite cantankerous. You been having trouble?"

"Oh, nothing to speak of," Slade replied, "but I'd like to see him."

"Ain't much to look at," replied the keeper. "The girls at the Widow Maker are easier on the eyes, but the sheriff's safer. Here's a key if you happen to come in late. I don't usually hand 'em out to strangers, but a man who forks a horse like that one has to be all right. A good horse with brains don't nuzzle the ear of a jigger who ain't what he should be. I've handled 'em too long not to know."

Slade thanked the keeper, who said his name was Lije Ballard, and left the stable satisfied that Shadow had nothing to worry about.

Passing a broad expanse of plate glass bearing the legend Widow Maker in red, Slade had no difficulty locating the sheriff's office which occupied a large room in the front of a solid-looking building housing the county jail.

Sheriff Ezra Bascomb proved to be a stocky old man with a drooping mustache. His face wore a stern expression but the corners of his mouth quirked upward and Slade sensed a twinkle in the depths of his pale eyes. He looked a bit surprised as The Hawk's tall figure loomed in the doorway but his nod was cordial enough.

"Well, son, what can I do for you?" he asked.

Slade told him tersely. The sheriff stared and tugged his mustache.

"Black handkerchiefs cut with eyeholes," he repeated. "Looks like the hellions might have belonged to the infernal Dawn Riders. What do you think?"

"I'm not prepared to say," Slade replied. "About all I know of the Dawn Riders is what old Sancho, the herder, told me, and he struck me as being a rather imaginative individual."

"He'd have had to use his imagination

overtime to tell you too much about the devils," Sheriff Bascomb growled. "They're about as salty, vicious and smart a bunch of owlhoots as ever operated in the Nueces country, and that's saying considerable. From the way you say they worked things, I'd say that pack belonged to the Dawn Riders, all right. And you killed two of them? Gentlemen, hush! A mighty good chore, though, no matter who the devil they were. Yes, I'll ride down there and bring 'em in. Should be able to make it by dark, and there's a full moon tonight."

"Suppose you'll want to hold an inquest?" Slade asked as he rose to go.

"Oh, sure," replied the sheriff. "No sense in it, but it's expected. I'll take old Sancho's word for what happened. I know him and he's a trustworthy coot even if he is a Mexican. Don't need to ask you to stick around; you'll stay here, all right. So long, it's been nice to have known you."

"Now just what do you mean by that?" Slade asked, pausing in the doorway.

"I mean," the sheriff replied grimly, "that you're good as dead right now!"

SIX

Slade chuckled as he headed for the Widow Maker and something to eat. The sheriff had a peculiar sense of humor, he reflected. However he did not discount the warning the old peace officer implied by his apparently facetious remark. It dovetailed nicely with what he had already heard, and, incidentally, experienced, relative to the Dawn Riders.

But El Halcon had gone up against too many shrewd and vicious outfits to be particularly perturbed by the prospect ahead of him.

As he strolled along the crowded street, Slade pondered with some amusement the unenviable reputation he enjoyed in some quarters. He had frequently worked under cover without revealing his Ranger connections. As a result, there were quite a few folks, including some puzzled sheriffs, who maintained that if El Halcon wasn't an owlhoot he missed being one by the skin of his teeth. Slade did nothing to discourage this erroneous viewpoint, having learned that at times it was to his advantage to be thought on the wrong side or riding close to the border of outlaw land. To those who knew him to be a Texas Ranger his name was almost legend and his exploits in the cause of law and order were spoken of with an admiration almost amounting to awe. "The smartest and most fearless Ranger of them all!" That's what was said by people who should know what they were talking about.

And of El Halcon it was said, by all who knew him, "The singingest man in Texas, and the fastest gunhand in the whole Southwest." Somewhat of an exaggeration, Slade felt. In fact, however, both statements came darn close to being gospel truth.

The Widow Maker proved to be a big saloon and doing plenty of business. Four drink jugglers were busy at the long mirror blazing bar. There was a dance floor with more than a few short-skirted, good-looking girls serving as partners for cowboys and *vaqueros* who thumped boots in time with the music provided by a very good Mexican orchestra.

There were three roulette wheels, all spinning, a faro bank, several dice tables and half a dozen others occupied by poker players who said little and paid scant attention to what was going on around them. There were also tables for the convenience of hungry patrons. A lunch counter catered to the wants of those who placed a higher premium on time than comfort.

Pottering about the far end of the bar was a huge man with little smiling eyes, a handlebar mustache and a cherubic countenance who nodded pleasantly to Slade as he found a place at the bar nearby. Slade surmised correctly that he was Border Shift Brewster, the owner.

Border Shift was wondrously fat, but from the lightness of his movements Slade shrewdly suspected that under the fat were great slabs of iron-hard muscle.

A cheerful bartender with a prodigious mustache and humorous eyes demanded that he name his pizen and sloshed a glass full to the brim. Slade sipped his drink and gave the room a once-over. Typical cow country saloon, to an extent, he decided. However, there were a number of customers who were doubtless from the oil fields, to which their laced boots, spattered with mud, and smudged shirts attested. All appeared cheerful, and peaceful enough, which, Slade knew, could be deceptive. Such a place always had plenty of dynamite in reserve. His attention was attracted to a nearby poker table at which an argument appeared to be getting underway; voices were rising and growing angry. Finally a big cowboy jumped to his feet with an oath and stood glaring at the other players. It wasn't hard to see that he would welcome trouble.

Border Shift Brewster stepped lightly to the table and tapped the belligerent one on the shoulder.

"Take it easy, son, take it easy!" he cautioned in a high-pitched but mellifluous voice.

The cowboy whirled at the touch. "Keep your fat paws off me, you lard tub, before I bust you one," he growled, drawing back his hand menacingly.

A dimpled fist whipped over and landed on the big puncher's jaw with a resounding smack. Down he went with a crash that set the hanging lamps to dancing. Cursing, he scrambled to his feet and rushed. Border Shift hit him again, with graceful ease, and down he went again, blood spurting from his cut lips. But again he came off the floor, raging, and went for his gun.

Border Shift's hand flashed across his vast middle. The cowboy stiffened, gripping the handle of his Colt. He was looking squarely into a black muzzle. Border Shift's speculative glance travelled up and down his form.

"Five-foot-eleven-inches should give plenty of head room," he remarked pensively.

"Border Shift runs the undertaking establishment, too," the bartender said breathlessly over Slade's shoulder. "He's measuring Butch for a coffin!"

The cowboy evidently understood perfectly what Border Shift meant; he whitened visibly.

"I didn't mean nothin', Border Shift," he mumbled thickly. "I'm sorry."

"You might have been sorrier," Border Shift observed as he holstered his gun. "Let's have a drink on it."

They had the drink together and the cowhand went back to his game, his lips puffed, and decidedly subdued. Border Shift caught Slade's eye and walked over to join him.

"Stranger hereabouts, aren't you?" he remarked pleasantly. "Don't mind the boys. They get a mite ringy now and then but I can usually tone 'em down."

"So I noticed," Slade replied dryly. "You appear able to handle them."

"Well, son," Border Shift replied in a fatherly way, "when you're drug up in the Border country saloon business like I was, you learn to handle men, and yourself, or you don't last. Times when you need to be gentle, times when you have to be tough. Getting along depends on proper timing. Let's have a drink on it.

"Yes, things are sort of lively since the big

oil strike over to the east," Border Shift remarked as they discussed the whiskey. "This used to be an easy-going pueblo with nothing much happening, but not any more. Folks have been pouring in from all over and we get all kinds. Keeps a feller on his toes. I'm making money, but I sort of think I liked things the way they used to be better. This sort of goings-on is all right when you're young, but when the years begin creeping up on you it sort of jostles you. I'm beginning to hanker for peace and quiet, and I ain't getting either."

Border Shift made the last remark in a mournful voice, but there was a gleam in his eye that belied it. Slade had a notion that Border Shift really liked the turbulent atmosphere.

"Much trouble?" he asked casually.

"Oh, nothing overly serious, so far," Border Shift replied. "A rukus now and then but nothing I'm not able to handle. Not bad here in town, but there's been plenty elsewhere. Widelooping and robbing and killings. Sheriff Bascomb is sort of beside himself of late. But what can you expect, with every owlhoot from here to the Big Bend and the Panhandle hustling in for pickings. Always this way when there's some sort of a strike in a section. Used to be mostly gold but now oil is sort of taking over, and I got a feeling it brings in an even saltier crowd. Yep, we've been getting some up-and-comin' gents hereabouts of late."

His glance suddenly centered on the swinging doors. "Here comes one I wouldn't want to tangle with," he remarked, lowering his voice.

The newcomer was indeed worthy of a second glance. He was a very tall man, almost as tall as Slade, broad of shoulder and lean of waist. He was rather handsome in a rugged, big-featured way with flashing dark eyes and a well-formed mouth.

It was his dress, however, that caught Slade's attention. He wore a long black coat, immaculately creased, black trousers and a black string tie. His highly polished boots were also black, as was his broad-brimmed "J.B." Only the snow of his ruffled shirt front and a flowered vest relieved the soberness of his garb.

"Gambler?" Slade asked.

"Nope, a ranchowner, name of Steve Gore," Border Shift replied. "About a year back, before the oil strike, he showed up and bought the Bradded L down to the southwest from old Isaiah Dwyer and has made a tip-top spread of it. I asked him once why he dressed like he always does

74

when he comes to town. He said he wore that kind of clothes for so long he doesn't feel dressed up without them. Was a dealer on Mississippi River steamboats for years, he said."

"Looks the part, all right," Slade conceded.

Gore apparently wore no gun but as he passed, with a nod to Border Shift, El Halcon's keen eyes detected a slight bulge over his left armpit. He felt pretty sure that a shoulder holster snugged there. He noted, too, that when Gore found a vacant table and sat down with his profile to the bar, he took a chair that faced the door.

"Quiet sort," resumed Border Shift. "Has a drink or two, dances with one of the girls now and then, and plays a good hand of cards but won't deal."

"Won't deal?"

"Nope," answered Border Shift. "One day one of the boys asked him why he always passed the deal. Gore smiled a little, took a deck and made those cards change spots and color, disappear and come back and do about everything but talk.

" 'See?' he said."

"I guess everybody saw, all right," Slade chuckled. "Those riverboat dealers are mighty deft with the pasteboards."

"They are," Border Shift agreed emphatically, "and I reckon Gore figured somebody might know that and get to wondering, if he happened to win considerable. I rather like the jigger, though there's some that don't."

"Why?" Slade asked.

"Well," explained Border Shift, "Gore is sort of close-mouthed and keeps to himself, and he works Mexicans and some Yaquis on his spread. When he came here he tried to hire some hands, but there weren't none available, so he went down to Mexico and come back with a bunch."

"Don't see why anybody should hold that against him, especially under the circumstances," Slade commented.

"I don't, either," nodded Border Shift, "but you know how some folks are in the Border country. His boys are all well-behaved and quiet. Couple of them over on the dance floor right now. I wouldn't want better customers."

"It's what a man is, not where he comes from," Slade observed.

"Glad you feel the same as I do about such things," said Border Shift. "Let's have a drink on it."

"As I rode to town I passed a big ranch-house in a grove, close to the trail," Slade remarked.

"Arn Harvey's place, the Diamond H," Border Shift instantly replied. "Son, if you're looking for a job of riding in this section, amble down and see him. Wouldn't be surprised if he'd put you on, pretty sure of it, in fact. Everybody's short-handed hereabouts of late — lots of the boys gone over to make big money in the oil field. And you couldn't work for a finer man, him or Miles Pacer who owns the Booger F next to the Diamond H holdings."

He paused, looked contemplative. "Funny story tied up with Arn Harvey and Miles Pacer," he added. "Like to hear it?"

Slade nodded and listened to a somewhat sketchy parallel of what Sancho Rojas related the night before, doubtless from the viewpoint of Arn Harvey and devoid, of course, of Sancho's personal experiences. He was interested to note, however, that in the main the two versions agreed.

Suddenly Border Shift stopped speaking and looked Slade up and down with his bright little eyes.

"Say!" he exclaimed in injured tones, "I came over to try and draw you out a bit — I like to keep tab on strangers who come in my place — find out who you are and where you come from, and so on, and here I've been spilling my guts all over the place and you ain't said a thing! How'd you do it?"

Border Shift didn't know it, but he was not the first to remark on Walt Slade's peculiar ability to lead the other man into doing all the talking.

"How the devil did you do it?" Border Shift repeated.

"By listening, I suppose," Slade smiled.

"Uh-huh, reckon that's it," Border Shift agreed. "Yep, I expect that's the answer. Let's have a drink on it."

"Okay," Slade conceded, "and then I want to get something to eat. Too much redeye on an empty stomach isn't good."

"Reckon so," Border Shift conceded. "I ain't never noticed it, though. Let's have — wait, we already got one."

"Getting back to your reason for visiting me," Slade remarked, "there's really not much to learn about me."

He supplied his name, adding, "And it's the one I got at the christening. I rode over from the west."

"Fine!" chuckled Border Shift as they shook hands. "Now I know everything. His name's Slade and he rode over from the west! No matter, though, I've sort of cottoned to you, son, and I don't cotton to everybody. Take that corner table while I

78

tell the cook to send you the best in the house."

A little later, Border Shift remarked to his head bartender, "There's something about that young feller that gets under your skin. He's been in here less than an hour and I feel as if I'd known him all my life."

"I've a notion he's a man to ride the river with," the bartender, an ex-cowhand, replied.

Border Shift nodded sober agreement to the highest compliment the rangeland can pay.

SEVEN

While he was enjoying a really excellent dinner, Slade noted that Steve Gore had finished eating. A moment later he paid his bill and walked out. Two young Mexicans immediately left the dance floor and followed him through the swinging doors.

A pretty close tie-up between the Bradded L owner and his hands, Slade reflected. Gore had merely gazed toward the dance floor a moment. That, however, apparently was enough.

After eating, Slade began to feel the effects of his sleepless night which he'd spent in the saddle. He approached Border Shift

79

and inquired about a room.

"Got a good one for you," said Border Shift. "And I'll send up a couple of swampers with a tub of hot water I reckon you can use, and a razor."

Thanks to the saloonkeeper's kindness, Slade enjoyed a bath and a shave. Then he lay down for a few hours of rest. He estimated that Sheriff Bascomb would not get back to town with the bodies of the outlaws until after midnight. He planned to be present when they were brought in.

As he drowsed, he reviewed the hectic events of the past twelve hours. In a way they were rather satisfactory. Unless the sheriff and Sancho Rojas were wrong in their beliefs, he managed to do for two of the notorious Dawn Riders. And the elimination of that pestiferous bunch was the object of his sojourn in the Nueces country.

"It's the sort of thing I hate to waste a Ranger on," Captain McNelty had said when he dispatched his lieutenant and aceman on his latest chore. "The local authorities should be able to take care of such brush-popping scum. But I've been getting a slew of letters asking for help. Particular one from an old jigger named Arn Harvey. I've known Harvey a long time and he's a good Injun. Try and contact him when you

80

get there. You can depend on what he tells you. A shrewd and salty proposition, too, and if Arn Harvey is asking for help things must be pretty bad. Would appear the situation has gotten plumb out of hand. The big oil interests drilling on the Ray land are complaining, too. Next thing they'll be going to the capital and asking why the devil they can't conduct their business without outlaw interference. And over there is always some darn politician ready to make the most of a thing like that. I don't want the outfit put on the spot; there are folks who would like to get rid of the Rangers, the only arm of the law the really big owlhoots are scared of."

"We'll try and keep 'em scared," Slade had replied cheerfully. "And," he'd added, "I've a notion we will."

Before he drifted off to sleep, Slade thought about Steve Gore a little. The Bradded L owner was certainly a bit out of the ordinary, and anything or anyone out of the ordinary interested El Halcon.

Slade slept longer than he'd intended, for he was very tired. When he descended to the Widow Maker he found the place in a great state of excitement.

"The sheriff just rode in with a couple of carcasses," Border Shift explained. "He says he thinks they belonged to the Dawn Riders, the owlhoot bunch that's been raising the devil and shoving a chunk under a corner. Judging from those black masks the hellions have got hanging around their necks, I figure maybe he could be right. If so, it's the first time anybody's been able to do for one of the sidewinders, let alone two. He didn't mention who did it, but whoever the gent is, he sure rates a vote of thanks from the community."

"Has he got the bodies at his office?" Slade asked. "Yes? I think I'll walk down there and take a look at them."

"I'll go with you," Border Shift offered. "Guess everybody will want to look the hellions over. Somebody might recognize them."

Slade thought so, too. The fact that the desperados went masked hinted that they might belong to some local outfit or hung around Sanders when they had nothing else to do.

When they arrived at the sheriff's office they found a constantly changing crowd. Man after man gazed at the stark forms on the floor and shook his head.

"This one does look a mite familiar to me," a man in a bartender's apron finally remarked, "but Yaquis all look alike; I couldn't say for sure."

"Only one hellion in this section works Yaquis," exclaimed a big, hulking individual at the edge of the crowd.

"That'll be enough of that kind of talk," Sheriff Bascomb warned.

"But it's true," the other insisted stubbornly. "The only man hereabouts who works Yaquis is Steve Gore."

"And what about Steve Gore?" said a voice behind him. He turned to face the Bradded L owner, who had just entered the room. He winced a little before Gore's glittering eyes but tried to bluster it out.

"Well, darn it, you do work Yaquis," he repeated, "and a man who'll work Yaquis and Mexicans —"

Steve Gore's hand shot out, gripped the other by the shirt front, shook him till his teeth rattled and hurled him back crashing against the wall.

"And if that isn't enough, fill your hand," he said grimly.

However, the other evidently decided it was enough; he slunk out.

"Sorry, Bascomb, I didn't come in to start a row," Gore said to the sheriff, "but that sort of talk can make for trouble."

"You're right," growled the sheriff, "and I'll put a stop to it or know the reason why."

Steve Gore pushed his way through the crowd. "Let me have a look at that pair," he said. "I don't think any of my boys would be mixed up in skullduggery, but a man can never be perfectly sure of what he hires, as everybody knows."

He gazed at the two dead men and shook his head. "Nope, never saw him before," he remarked, apropos of the Yaqui. "Nice shooting — square between the eyes. Who did it?"

Sheriff Bascomb jerked his head toward Slade, who was immediately the recipient of stares from all present. Steve Gore looked him up and down with a swift glance.

"And did you get the other one, too?" he asked. Slade nodded.

"A good chore, a darn good chore," Gore said. "Hope you get a chance at some more of the devils." He turned and left the room.

"I can't make that feller out," complained the sheriff, "but one thing is sure for certain, he's a cold proposition."

Nobody seemed inclined to dispute the statement.

"Well, that'll be all for tonight," said the sheriff. "I craves some shuteye. Inquest at two in the afternoon."

The crowd shuffled out, glancing curiously at El Halcon. Sheriff Bascomb motioned Slade to wait. Border Shift Brewster also remained.

"I brought Rojas back with me," the sheriff said after he had shut the door. "He's up at the Rosalita, having a drink with some of his Mexican friends. Take him to your place for the night, Border Shift; I want him to last till after the inquest, anyhow. Glad to see you're still alive, Slade; try and stay that way till two o'clock. If you drink much of that snake juice this fat hellion takes money for, you won't, though. It would pizen a Gila Monster. That joint of his is sure named right."

"Guess that's right," agreed Border Shift. "Let's go have a drink on it."

"Don't mind if I do," the sheriff accepted.

Sheriff Bascomb locked the door and they repaired to the Widow Maker to sample the snake juice. After two glasses the sheriff appeared little the worse for wear.

"Now we'll go up to the Rosalita and get Rojas," he said. "Slade, you can bring him back here for the night. Then I am going to bed."

As they started up the street the muffled boom of a shot sounded not far away. "Now what the devil!" growled the sheriff, lengthening his stride.

A little distance up the street a crowd was

gathering in front of a saloon.

"The Rosalita," muttered the sheriff and pushed through the swinging doors, Slade at his heels.

Inside the *cantina* all was confusion. Dance floor girls were squealing, men were cursing in two languages. On the floor lay a man whose face was streaked with blood.

"Good God!" exclaimed the sheriff, "it's Rojas!"

Slade knelt beside the old herder and with deft fingers examined an ugly gash just above the hairline.

"Creased," he told the sheriff. "I don't think he's badly hurt. Somebody get me water and a clean cloth."

The water and cloth were quickly forthcoming. Slade washed the blood from Sancho's face and cleansed the wound. Sancho groaned, rolled his head from side to side and opened his eyes. He looked dazed at first, then a flash of recognition crossed his face.

"Capitan!" he murmured, "they do not give up easily."

"Looks like you're right," Slade agreed soberly. "Now you take it easy for a bit. How do you feel?"

"Not too bad," Sancho replied. "My head aches and I am a trifle dizzy, but I do not think I have taken a serious hurt."

The old man was full of a sort of surly courage that would never admit defeat. He insisted on getting up. Slade supported him till he ceased to sway and was firm on his feet.

"And now somebody tell us what happened," said the sheriff.

A dozen voices answered at once, but the sheriff singled out a portly Mexican who was the owner.

"You tell us, Felipe," he directed.

"Somebody stuck a gun through the window over there that opens on the alley," Felipe replied. "A shot was fired and Sancho who was sitting at the nearby table, fell to the floor. I ran to the window but could see nobody; it is dark out there."

The sheriff nodded. "Regulation drygulching," he growled. "Did you see anything, Sancho?"

"A flash of something white," replied the herder. "Doubtless it saved my life, for I instinctively started to rise from my chair."

"A flash of white?" Slade repeated. "What did it look like?"

"I would say," Sancho replied, "a shirt front."

Slade glanced at the sheriff. The old peace officer's brows were knit.

"Not many folks hereabouts wear white shirts, except bartenders and storekeepers," he observed. "You sure it was a shirt front, Sancho?"

"No, *Señor* Sheriff, I am not sure," Sancho replied. "I got but a glimpse of it, but it looked like a shirt front."

"Okay, we'll let it go at that," Bascomb said. "Come along, now, and we'll rout out the doctor and have your head tied up. Mustn't take chances with it."

"It is nothing," Sancho protested, but the sheriff was insistent.

"Don't want a man cashing in because of neglect," he said. "Come along. Then you can take him to the Widow Maker, Slade, and put him to bed. I don't think anybody will take a shot at him there."

The old frontier doctor also made light of the wound. "But another inch to the right and he'd have busted up a dull day for Border Shift, the undertaker," he said. "There, that ought to hold you," he added, giving the bandage a final pat.

The sheriff went home to bed. Slade took Sancho to the Widow Maker and assisted him up the stairs. After making sure he was resting easily he went back to the saloon and joined Border Shift at the bar.

Border Shift shot him an exasperated

glance. "And you never said a word about doing for those two devils," he complained in injured tones. "You sure don't talk!"

"Well, you could hardly expect me to bring up the subject," Slade smiled reply. "And it was logical to believe that you'd hear about it soon, anyhow."

"Guess that's right," admitted Border Shift. "Let's have a drink on it."

"But why did they want to kill Sancho Rojas?" he wondered as the glasses were filled. "That old coot's been around here thirty years and never did no harm to anybody."

That was a question to which Slade earnestly desired the answer. He was still pondering it when he went to bed to finish his interrupted sleep.

EIGHT

The inquest the following afternoon was brief. The coroner's jury did not even take the trouble to leave the box to arrive at a verdict. The foreman 'lowed that Slade did a darn good chore and a favor to the community and suggested that it would be a good notion for him to go out and shoot some more. The general consensus was that the dead outlaws had been members of the notorious Dawn Riders and Slade received some well-meant advice to the effect that it wouldn't be a bad notion for him to trail his rope out of the section.

"Those hellions will be out to even the score, son," an old cattleman said. "You came well out of it. Don't play your luck too strong."

Slade thanked his well wishers and didn't take their advice.

A different sort of advice was voiced by Steve Gore, who came to town for the inquest and approached Slade in the Widow Maker.

"Don't let the hellions run you out," the Bradded L owner said. "Once a man starts on the run he has trouble getting out of the habit. I know. I tried it once, when I was quite young and had trouble with a pretty bad bunch that played on one of the boats. Got so I was scared of my own shadow. Everybody who looked in my direction I figured was one of the bunch after me. About a year of that and I said the devil with it, I'm going back and let those hellions try to do their darndest. I went back, got a job dealing right on the boat where I knew they always played. Three of them came in and sat down at my table.

" 'Why, hello, Steve, where you been keeping yourself?' one of them said. They'd forgotten all about the row we had and never even mentioned it. That taught me never to run from trouble. It's just like a cloud that makes an awful big shadow coming toward you, but once it's past you see it's nothing but a shadow."

With a friendly nod he walked to a table and ordered something to eat. Slade regarded his broad back with interest.

Steve Gore undoubtedly was a bit out of the ordinary.

Slade had a talk with Border Shift Brewster. "I'd like to ask you a favor," he said.

"Shoot!" said Border Shift. "It's granted already — anything you ask. What do you want me to do?"

"I want you to put Sancho Rojas to work here where you can keep an eye on him," Slade explained. "If he goes back to that cabin, his life won't be worth a busted cartridge."

"I've a notion you've got the right of it," said Border Shift. "Okay, I'll put him to work in the kitchen and tell the boys to watch out for him. He'll be safe there. I've got a salty bunch working for me and if anybody comes in here looking for trouble, they'll get it till it runs out of their ears. Don't worry about Sancho, he'll be okay. Let's have a drink on it."

The inquest had taken but a short while and the hour was still early. Slade abruptly arrived at a decision which he proceeded to act upon. He got the rig on Shadow and rode south.

Slade did not expect any trouble in the course of his ride to the Diamond H ranchhouse. Certainly nobody knew he intended to visit Arn Harvey — he hadn't known it himself until just before he started out. Nevertheless, he did not relax his vigilance. For the most part the road was across open prairie, but about half-way to his destination, the trail writhed down into a deep hollow where it was heavily brush grown on both sides, providing sufficient cover for a hundred drygulchers, and until he had climbed the far sag and was in the open again, El Halcon was indeed very much on the alert. The spot was perfect for an ambush.

As he approached the Diamond H ranchhouse he observed two men sitting on the veranda. One was a big bushy-haired oldster with a rugged, weatherbeaten face. Slade rightly judged that he was Arn Harvey.

Old Arn waved a greeting. "Light off, cowboy, and cool your saddle," he shouted hospitably. Slade nodded his acceptance of the invitation and turned off the trail. As he dismounted by the steps, Arn Harvey suddenly sat bolt upright in his chair.

"Say!" he exclaimed, "you must be the feller Bill and Pete were talking about when they rode in from town. Must be; couldn't be two alike. Your name Slade?"

"So I've been told," Slade replied with a smile.

Harvey turned to his companion, a tall broad-shouldered and very good looking man with twinkling black eyes, a dark complexion and a smiling mouth.

"Miles, it's him!" he exclaimed. "The young feller who did for two of those dad-blamed Dawn Riders! Come up and set, son, and tell us all about it."

He whooped for a wrangler. "Take that horse and put it in the stable," he ordered. "This gent's staying for supper."

Slade gave Shadow the word and the wrangler led him away. Old Arn followed him with his eye.

"Some cayuse!" he said. "Never saw a finer looking one."

"He'll do," Slade agreed as he mounted the steps.

"What's your front handle, son?" Harvey asked. "This is Mr. Miles Pacer who owns the Booger F next to my holdings."

Miles Pacer acknowledged the introduction and shook hands with a good grip. His voice was pleasantly modulated. Slade decided he was doubtless a man of some education. He sat down and fished out the makin's. Harvey and Pacer regarded him expectantly as he rolled a cigarette with the slim fingers of his left hand.

Knowing what they were waiting for, Slade regaled them with an account of the previous day's happenings, refraining, however, from making any mention of what Sancho Rojas told him concerning the tragic treasure hunt in which he, unknown to Arn Harvey, had participated. Old Arn clucked admiringly.

"And you did for two of the devils!" he marvelled, and proceeded to ask the question for which Slade didn't have the answer. "But why would they want to kill that poor old Mexican?"

After a few more minutes of desultory conversation, Miles Pacer suddenly rose to his feet.

"Where you going?" asked Harvey.

"I'm heading back to the spread," Pacer replied.

"Thought you were going to stay for supper?"

"I'd intended to, but I got to thinking," Pacer explained. "I want to have another look at that stretch of rocks and prickly pear just this side of San Cajo. That's where we lost the trail of the last bunch of stock we lost, you know. I have a feeling there's a way through that mess somewhere. I'll get an early start in the morning and comb it carefully."

"That's the goshawfulest, lonesomest and thorniest pasture to be hit south of the Nueces, and that's saying plenty," Harvey growled. "It curves all the way around San Cajo and gets worse the farther you go. No wonder you lost the trail. But those danged owlhoots seem to know ways through everything, and they could drive an elephant across a snowbank and not leave a track."

He turned to Slade. "Miles and some of his boys were trying to track down a bunch of hellions who widelooped some of his steers, night before last," he explained. "We were just talking about it when you rode up."

"Much trouble of that sort hereabouts?" Slade asked.

"Too much during the past year, ever since those infernal Dawn Riders, as somebody named 'em, started operating in the section," Harvey answered. "We've all been catching it, me and Pacer the worst of all, being down here to the southwest and not

95

so far from the Rio Grande. Yes, everybody's been losing stock. Funny, though, the feller that's lost the least, according to what he says, is Steve Gore whose holding is closest of all to the river. You'd think he'd be the biggest loser. Funny, ain't it?"

"Yes, very funny," Pacer remarked dryly.

Old Arn tugged his mustache and did not comment. Pacer said nothing more relative to the matter. He turned to Slade.

"Riding back to town tonight, Mr. Slade?" he asked casually.

"He ain't," old Arn stated definitely. "He's going to stay for supper and spend the night here. I want to talk to him. You rode over from the west, I believe you said, son. I'd like to hear about conditions over there. If things keep going like they have been of late, I'm liable to pull up stakes and go looking for a better section."

"You're sort of getting along to be contemplating such a move," smiled Pacer.

"Oh, I don't know," Harvey replied cheerfully. "I'm just pushing sixty and that ain't so old. I can still fork a cayuse and ride with the boys. Not that I don't feel it a mite sometimes," he admitted with a chuckle. "Old bones get sore easier than young ones. Ain't bothered with rheumatism or anything like that, so far, and I still got most of my teeth."

Pacer laughed. "Hope I'm good as you are when I get to be your age," he said.

"You got a long ways to go," answered Harvey.

"But the way things are going hereabouts of late, I'm liable not to last that long," Pacer observed pessimistically. "I never did like to hear lead whistle close by. Well, so long. I'll get my horse. If you ride to town in the morning, Mr. Slade, I may see you there later in the day. Got to arrange for some stock cars."

"Yes, I'll be riding back in the morning," Slade said. "Chances are I'll be in the Widow Maker for supper. Perhaps we can get together there."

"I'll try and make it," Pacer promised. With a pleasant nod he headed for the stable.

"A darn nice feller," commented Harvey. "I've got to liking him considerable and he comes around frequent. May be seeing even more of him after a while," he added with a chuckle. "I think he sort of likes my girl Audrey."

"Does she like him?" Slade asked with a smile.

"Darned if I know," old Arn confessed.

"Don't see any reason why she shouldn't. As I said, he's a nice feller, and nice looking, a hard worker and sober. What more could a girl ask of a man?"

"Hard to tell," Slade answered, an amused light in his gray eyes. "You never can tell about a woman."

"That's so," conceded Harvey. "My wife was one of the prettiest girls in the section, and she took up with a homely shorthorn like me."

Abruptly his stern mouth was very tender and there was a wistful look in his faded eyes.

"You're a widower, Mr. Harvey?" Slade asked gently.

"That's right," Arn replied. "She died a couple of years back. Hit me mighty hard. But the Lord giveth and the Lord taketh away. Blessed be the name of the Lord!"

Walt Slade bowed his head to the old man's simple piety.

For some time they sat smoking in silence, each busy with his own thoughts. Suddenly Harvey exclaimed, "Here comes Audrey now!"

A girl mounted on a mettlesome roan was riding up the driveway. In front of the steps she dropped the split reins to the ground and dismounted lithely.

One look at her was enough to convince Slade that Harvey had uttered no idle boast when he declared his wife had been one of the prettiest girls in the section. Audrey Harvey certainly never got her big blue eyes, her softly brown, curly hair, her pert little nose and her sweetly turned red mouth from her father. And yet, there was no denying their resemblance. There was something in the set of her firm little chin that was reminiscent of old Arn's stubborn jut, and the expression of the eyes was similar. Slade was of the opinion also that she might possibly have her share of the famous Harvey temper.

"Hello, honey," Arn greeted her as she ran up the steps. "Want you to know Mr. Walt Slade who is having supper with us and staying for the night. Slade, this is my daughter Audrey."

The girl smiled brightly and extended a slim little sun-golden hand over which Slade bowed with courtly grace. Her glance was frank as she looked him up and down and there was no question but that the blue eyes mirrored approval.

"Is he going to work for us?" she asked her father, her voice low and musical.

"Well, I haven't asked him yet, but I hope he says yes when I do," old Arn chuckled.

"That is," he added mischievously, "if you don't object."

"I won't object," she declared with vigor. "He'll be a welcome relief. Most of our hands, Mr. Slade, are about Dad's age and just as cantankerous. The rest are tongue-tied in a woman's presence."

"Maybe it's because they never get a chance to put in a word edgewise," her father grunted. "What about it, Slade?"

"Well," Slade smiled, "if more men would listen to what women tell them there'd be a lot less trouble in the world."

Audrey laughed merrily and clapped her hands. "Dad, he's sensible, too," she said. "Please sign him on."

"I'll do my best," old Arn promised with a chuckle. "But you'd better get ready to eat. Put something on beside those darn pants. I like a woman to look like a woman."

Audrey glanced down at her worn but trimly fitting Levis. "Dad's old-fashioned," she said. "If he had his way he'd have me riding side-saddle. I wonder whoever started that ridiculous habit, anyhow."

"I have heard," Slade said, smiling broadly, "that the custom was brought into fashion by a certain French princess who had a deformed leg."

"Well, if that's the case, I think I can stick

to overalls," Audrey giggled and went into the house.

NINE

A little later the cook let out a stentorian bellow and Harvey led the way to the dining room, into which the Diamond H hands were already streaming. As Audrey said, most of them were grizzled old waddies but there were several fresh-faced youngsters who did not seem to be exactly speechless, even after Audrey arrived wearing something beyond masculine description, but which Slade thought was extremely becoming and feminine enough to comply with even old Arn's exacting requirements.

Slade was introduced to the assemblage and old Arn rattled off a string of names. An observant individual, he noted that afterward when Slade had occasion to address a man, he invariably called him by the right name.

After the meal, a good one, was finished, Slade and Harvey repaired to the big living room and smoked and talked. Audrey sat by the lamp and read a book, or pretended to.

Finally the talk got around to the great oil strike on the Ray ranch, only a few miles to the east.

"Ever since I was a boy, and long before that, folks have been digging in this section for buried treasure," Harvey remarked. "Reckon the old-timers would be mighty surprised to learn how folks finally dug it up.

"But they had to dig a sight deeper than the old fellers could with a pick and spade," he added with a chuckle.

He was silent a moment and his eyes grew somber. "Yes, there was a lot of digging, and some of it didn't come to any good," he said. "Digging for buried gold cost me my two brothers. It's quite a yarn. Like to hear it?"

Slade heard Audrey sigh resignedly. Evidently old Arn never missed an opportunity to repeat the tale. He stifled a grin and nodded. He was getting into a position to sympathize with Audrey.

For the third time he listened to the story of hidden treasure and its surprising aftermath. He was interested to note that as to salient points, Arn Harvey's account did not differ from the others which he had heard.

"And you couldn't find the place when you went hunting for it?" he commented.

Harvey shook his head. "Never looked for it but once — that time with the county surveyor — but I'm sure I covered all the ground. Reckon the darn map must have been wrong. Wait a minute."

He rummaged around in a table drawer and drew forth a yellowed parchment.

"Here she is," he announced. "See what you can make of it."

Slade took the map and examined it. He peered at the point where the bisecting lines crossed and read the legend, "My Treasure." For several minutes he studied the document in silence.

"It looks authentic, all right," he said musingly. "But this wording is unusual — My treasure! Has almost a sentimental sound. And seldom does such a map, doubtless drawn for purposes of reference or to guide someone trusted to the spot, outline precisely the location of whatever was hidden. Generally the designation is vague and often requires a key to determine it. Not that this isn't to a degree quite vague. The tie points are noted as — two chimney rocks a thousand paces apart and a mountain. The mountain is not named and there is nothing to identify it as San Cajo. I've a notion that whoever your brothers got this map from also added some verbal information."

"Could be," conceded Harvey. "My brother Sid got it from an old Mexican who got it from a sick sailor who got it from the devil knows who. Maybe he did tell Sid something that isn't written down. Well, it caused plenty of trouble, anyhow. The devil with it!"

He thrust the parchment back in the drawer. "Well, son, are you going to sign up with us?" he asked. "I can use another top hand. And somebody intelligent to talk with now and then," he added.

"You mean somebody intelligent to talk to," his daughter remarked.

"There must be something wrong with her this evening," old Arn commented. "I never knew her to keep quiet for so long a stretch. But you'll catch it after I go to bed, son; prepare to have your ears bent plumb out of shape. And what do you say about signing up?"

"Mr. Harvey, I thank you very much for the offer," Slade replied. "I think I'll take you up on it, but first I want to ride to town in the morning and make sure old Sancho Rojas is okay; I sort of feel responsible for him."

"Fine," said Harvey. "We'll let it go at that. And now I'm going to bed. You youngsters can sit up all night and gab if you want to, but old bones crave rest. Put him in the first room to the right at the head of the stairs, Audrey."

He nodded to Slade, patted Audrey's shoulder and clumped up the stairs. Audrey sighed dolefully and shook her head.

"I've listened to that story at least fifty times," she declared. "Dad never misses a chance to tell it. Personally I think it's all so much rubbish. I don't believe there's anything of value to be found on that sand flat, wherever it is, do you?"

"I'm not so sure," Slade replied quietly. "There may be something of very great value there. I'm not prepared to say for sure just yet, but I hope to be able to later."

Audrey looked at him expectantly, but he answered, "That's all I care to say at present, and keep what I have said under the hat you don't wear."

"I will," she promised, "if for no other reason, just to show you that a woman can keep a secret."

"Oh, they can, some secrets," he smiled.

"You have an unusual way of talking for a — cowhand out of work."

"Perhaps, for a cowhand out of work," Slade agreed.

The big eyes regarded him very seriously. "I wonder," she said, "if you are really out of work?"

"Now what do you mean by that?" he asked.

"Nothing in particular," she replied. "It's a woman's prerogative to wonder about a man."

"Prerogative implies a distinct superiority," he commented. "So by reverse analogy, a man is not accorded that privilege?"

"I'd answer that by saying that in my opinion a man very seldom avails himself of that privilege; he usually takes a woman for granted."

"And sometimes he suffers a rude awakening, and a shock to his vanity," Slade chuckled.

She laughed and deftly changed the subject. "Getting back to the treasure story," she said, "I think the most amazing part of the whole affair is Miles Pacer showing up here after all those years."

"But a perfectly logical development," Slade pointed out.

"Yes, I suppose so," she conceded, "but just the same I feel it borders on the fantastic."

"Truth often does."

She nodded. "Anyhow he's a good neighbor and there is no doubt but the Booger F was rightfully his by inheritance. That's the way Dad felt about it."

106

"Your father seems to think well of him."

"Oh, there's no reason why he shouldn't," she replied. "But Dad looks on every presentable male as a potential husband for me. He's old-fashioned and thinks when a girl is approaching twenty-three she's on the verge of becoming an old maid."

"I gather from your remarks that you don't exactly share your father's matrimonial aspirations relative to Mr. Pacer," he observed.

"I certainly do not," she replied emphatically. "He seems nice, but I don't think I could stand that eternal smile of his as a steady diet. I prefer a man who frowns now and then, even at me."

"I think it would be hard ever to frown at you," he chuckled.

"Oh, you haven't seen all my moods," she disagreed. "Like all women, I have claws."

"And smart enough, I'll wager, to know when to keep them sheathed."

"But it takes a great deal of forbearance at times."

Slade laughed again. "You are an outstanding refutation of the contention that beauty and brains don't go together," he said.

"Beauty is dependent on the personal reaction of the beholder," she answered, "and

I'm not at all sure as to the brains, especially after tonight."

"Why tonight?"

The blue eyes met his squarely. "Because in the last analysis, a woman is always swayed by her emotions, not her judgment. But enough talk. I'm keeping you up all hours and you must have had a hard day."

TEN

Slade left the Diamond H ranchhouse early the following morning. He chuckled as he thought of Audrey and wondered a bit uneasily if he hadn't at last perhaps met his match. She was certainly out of the ordinary. She had had an effect on him that was unusual, to put it mildly. Beauty, brains, and everything else a woman needed. One thing he felt sure of, he wasn't going to forget her easily.

However, at the moment he had other things to think about besides big blue eyes and a trim little form. Before him were five miles of going through a country that might hold anything. Instinctively he kept to the side of the trail in the early morning shadow. For a couple of miles the terrain was open; then the trail dropped down a sag into the brush grown hollow he had noted the day before. At the crest of the rise he pulled up in the shadow and studied the trail ahead. It was utterly deserted and in the depths of the hollow was a curdling mist that accentuated the gloom the sun had not yet pierced. To all appearances there was nothing to worry about, but somehow Slade didn't feel just right about those shadowy and silent depths.

In men who ride much alone with danger as a constant stirrup companion there often develops a subtle sixth sense that warns of peril where apparently none exists; and in El Halcon this elusive quality was highly developed indeed. And now the silent monitor was setting up an unheard but very real clamor. Slade tried to tell himself it was but the effect caused by the uninviting prospect ahead, but his insistence was not very convincing. He was worried about that stretch of trail ahead and there was no sense in trying not to admit it. For minutes he sat motionless on his motionless horse, studying the hollow, trying to pierce the thick brush with his gaze, listening for any untoward sound.

Suddenly there was motion apparent in the depths below. From the brush on the right appeared several squat little shapes. Slade quickly identified them as a small herd of javelinas, the little wild pigs of the brush country. They nosed in the dust, started across the trail. Then abruptly the silence was broken by a hurricane of squeals that reached to the watcher on the crest. The javelinas whirled about and streaked back the way they had come. Almost instantly the last whisking tail had vanished in the brush to the right.

Slade stared at the again deserted trail, his black brows drawing together.

"Shadow, what the devil set those fellers off that way?" he wondered aloud. He knew that javelinas, like all pigs, were given to senseless panics; but just the same the animals had acted as if they saw or scented something that changed their minds for them and caused them to forgo their evident intention of crossing the trail to the chaparral growth on the far side. For another moment he sat staring into the hollow, then he abruptly turned Shadow and sent him into the growth on the left. A short distance from the trail he came upon a little cleared space where there was grass. He dismounted, dropping the split reins to the ground and flipped the bit out so the horse could graze in comfort.

"And don't go singing any songs," he cautioned. "If there is somebody down there and you let out a whinny, you'll give the whole thing away."

He wasn't much worried, however. Shadow was usually a very quiet horse.

The brush was thick and it was gloomy under the interlacing branches. Slade made slow progress down the slope, pausing often to peer and listen. He had reached the bottom of the sag when he heard a sound that tensed him to hairtrigger alertness; from somewhere ahead came the impatient stamp of a horse. For long minutes he did not move, but as no further sound reached his ears, he resumed his slow progress, angling toward the trail. Then he halted again. From a distance of only a few yards came a mutter of low voices. He waited again, then glided forward, careful to break no twig, to rustle no leaf. Another moment and he saw two shadowy figures lounging in the final fringe of brush next to the trail. The two men were talking together and their words reached him.

"Hellion should be showing any time now," one muttered. "And when he does, let him have it and good. Keep on shooting till he drops, and after he hits the ground. Don't take any chances, he's bad."

The other grunted an unintelligible response. Then both fell silent, their eyes fixed on the trail they could see while not being seen; evidently they were listening for the sound of hoofbeats coming down the sag.

Slade's face set in bleak lines and his gray eyes were icily cold. He felt a hot surge of anger as he gazed at the backs of the two killers. They were out to do murder. He would be justified in mowing them down where they stood. They didn't deserve any more chance than they intended to give him when, as they expected, he would appear riding down the trail.

But the code of the Rangers forbade such action. He was a peace officer and must conduct himself as one. The two murderous devils must be given a chance to surrender. Well, that might be to his advantage in the long run; their sort would often talk to save their own worthless necks, and if they could be induced to divulge information that would lead him to the brains of the organization then something really worth while would be accomplished, far more important than the wiping out of a couple of hired hands, as it were. He loosened his guns in their holsters and took another step forward to avoid a cluster of twigs that slightly obscured his view. And the unpredictable happened. He planted his foot on what appeared to be solid ground and wasn't; it was a badger hole filled with leaves smoothed over by the wind. Down went his leg, half-way up the calf. He floundered off balance, grabbed a branch to keep from falling. It broke with a crack like a pistol shot. The two drygulchers whirled at the sound, guns coming out.

Back and forth through the gloom spurted the red flashes. The air quivered to the reports. Slade reeled as a bullet grazed his forehead. Another drew blood from his left arm. A third burned a red streak across his left cheek. Then he lowered his smoking guns and peered at the two bodies sprawled on the dead leaves. He strode forward, ready for instant action; but the outlaws were as dead as the leaves on which they lay. Slade gave a quick glance around, listened a moment, then holstered his guns.

One of the dead men was a stocky individual with a face blotched and bloated by drink and the devil alone knew what other vices. His companion was a scrawny little rat of an individual with a reptilian mouth gashing his bloodless face and a nose that had been broken and driven in at the bridge. Otherwise, both were nondescript characters, typical Border scum, cruel, vicious, fearless but, Slade judged, as shy of brains as a terrapin is of feathers. The sort that could take orders and carry them out ruthlessly, and that was as far as they went.

Their pockets revealed nothing of significance aside from a large sum of money; their clothing was rangeland and ordinary, their guns regulation Colt Forty-fives. Rising to his feet, he listened a minute and was rewarded by the snort of a nervous horse nearby. It took him but a few minutes to locate the killers' mounts, good horses, but nothing outstanding about them. They bore Mexican brands that were meaningless so far as identification was concerned. The rigs were well worn but serviceable.

Slade reloaded his guns, leaned against a convenient tree and rolled a cigarette. After a few satisfying drags he turned and walked back to where he had left Shadow. Regaining the trail he rode down the sag and pulled up opposite where the bodies lay. Dismounting, he untied the two horses and lashed the bodies across their saddles. Then he bunched the reins in his hand and set out for town.

Citizens of Sanders stared as the grim cavalcade passed along the main street, but the look on Slade's face forbade questions. A crowd quickly gathered and followed at a discreet distance.

Slade pulled up before the sheriff's office,

dismounted and entered. Sheriff Bascomb was at his desk busy with some letters. He glanced up quickly.

"Well, now what?" he asked.

Slade sat down and rolled a cigarette before replying. Outside was a babble of voices.

"Couple more for your collection," he said when he had the brain tablet manufactured and going satisfactorily.

The sheriff stared. Then he got to his feet and hurried out. He returned a little later, regarded Slade a moment and shook his head.

"It would be easy to track you down by just following the empty bodies," he remarked. "What happened?"

Slade told him, briefly. The sheriff swore and shook his head again.

"No black masks on this pair?" he asked.

"None that I noticed," Slade replied.

"Just the same I'll bet a hatful of *pesos* they belonged to the same bunch as the other two. Still trying to even up the score, eh?"

"Would look that way," Slade admitted.

"And how long do you think your luck will hold out?"

Slade shrugged his broad shoulders. "So long as it does hold, I won't worry about it," he replied.

The sheriff nodded. "Well, anyhow you're thinning the hellions out a bit," he said. "And I don't think it's a very big bunch, not more than eight or ten at the outside, maybe not that many. Yes, you're thinning them out."

"Perhaps," Slade conceded, adding, "but the head of the outfit is still running around loose, and that sort of a head can grow another body mighty fast."

"You're right about that," the sheriff agreed. "Making business for the coroner, at least, and Border Shift Brewster should give you a cut; the county has to pay him for planting those sidewinders. Would be cheaper if you'd left them for the coyotes and buzzards."

"I brought them in on the faint chance that somebody might recognize them," Slade answered.

"I'll lay 'em out and let everybody have a look," Bascomb decided. He left the office and Slade heard him ordering the bodies unloaded and brought in. The procedure of a couple of nights before was repeated, but with equally barren results.

"Because of the report that your Dawn Riders always go masked, I was of the notion that it might be a local outfit," Slade remarked when they were left alone again. "However, it would appear that it isn't. That is at least so far as the rank and file go. Perhaps the hellion who's the big he-wolf of the pack is from the section."

Sheriff Bascomb shot him a keen glance then shrugged his shoulders. "You could be right," he admitted noncommittally.

"As I understand it, several times there have been robberies committed at ranches where money had just been received," Slade commented.

"That's right," agreed the sheriff.

"Which would lead one to think that somebody connected with the outfit is in a position to get information relative to local happenings," Slade added.

"Right again," the sheriff admitted.

"And something to think about," Slade observed, rising to his feet. "Well, I'm going over to the Widow Maker and get something to eat. Care to join me?"

"Okay," said the sheriff. "We'll stop at Doc Cooper's and tell him to take care of those carcasses and set an inquest for whenever he's of a mind to. Just a waste of time, but Doc feels he should do something to earn his pay as coroner."

When Slade and the sheriff entered the Widow Maker, a hush fell. Men turned to stare at the tall Hawk, but nobody approached him. Finally, however, Border Shift Brewster could stand it no longer. He came over to the table where Slade and the sheriff were awaiting their order.

"Slade," he said plaintively, "won't you please tell me what the devil happened? The boys are so darn curious they can't drink, and that's bad for business."

Slade chuckled, and told him. Border Shift shook his head in admiration.

"Well, you sure have raised hell and shoved a chunk under a corner since you landed here," he said. "Bascomb, you ought to make him a deputy. Let's have a drink on it."

Slade thought the twinkle that always seemed to lurk in the back of Sheriff Bascomb's frosty eyes was more than usually pronounced when he answered, "Maybe I will."

Border Shift went back to the bar; the crowd clustered about him. More glances were shot in Slade's direction, to the accompaniment of much wagging of heads.

"You're becoming considerable of a celebrity," observed the sheriff. "Hope everybody finds time to come to the funeral."

ELEVEN

After he finished eating, Sheriff Bascomb hurried off to confer with the coroner. Slade remained at the table, smoking and thinking. He felt that he had plenty to think about. He had come to the Nueces country with a definite purpose in view. So far he had merely become embroiled in what appeared to be a personal feud with some outfit that might be the Dawn Riders and then again might not. Undoubtedly he had irritated somebody. That is if that was the answer. He began to suspect that it wasn't. The first attempt on his life might be explained that way, but the second, coldly planned in advance and carried out with patience and plenty of forethought, he considered a different matter. It appeared that somebody was desperately anxious that he be removed from the scene. Why? Of course he may have been recognized as El Halcon with a reputation for horning in on good things, but he doubted if that, either, was the answer. Conditions being what they were in the section at the moment, there were plenty of good pickings to support more than one owlhoot bunch. He could have been spotted as a Texas Ranger, yes, but he was a bit dubious about even that being the explanation, at least so far as surface indications went. There must be some deep-seated reason for what amounted to an almost frantic effort to eliminate him immediately. And then there was the inexplicable problem that he felt was a component of the unresolved pattern: why was somebody so anxious to kill old Sancho Rojas? Slade was almost inclined to believe that Sancho might be right in his absurd contention that whoever heard the story from him of the ancient treasure hunt was slated for death. Ridiculous, of course, but Slade had a hunch that in some unexplained manner the old treasure hunt and its amazing aftermath were mixed up in the business. Seemed absurd, but it was something to ponder on.

Walt Slade had the reputation of being the most fearless and ablest of the Texas Rangers. It was also claimed by many that he had the fastest and most accurate gunhand in the Southwest. As to this last Slade himself was frankly doubtful. In his opinion there were plenty of men on the other side of the corral fence who were as fast or faster and just as sure shots. He was very likely right, but the difference lay in a faster mind and a better ability to size up a situation. The gun battle of the morning with the two drygulchers was an example. Both men had fired before he did, but in their eagerness to get in the first shot they had fired wildly. Slade, on the other hand, was set before he pulled trigger. As a result his first two shots found the mark. His quick mind weighed the chances and estimated them correctly. This was the real explanation of his uniform success in dealing with the outlaw fraternity. Mentally he was always one jump ahead of them.

Not that it was always a simple matter. He had gone up against men of far more than average intelligence, and he had an uneasy premonition that his present opponent, whoever the devil he was, could well be of a similar calibre.

He wondered, a bit uneasily, if old Arn Harvey might be in danger. Rather unlikely, though, he reasoned. What Harvey knew about the treasure hunt was common property and it was also known that he had failed to find the spot in question and had no desire to do so. It appeared that Sancho Rojas was the only living person who did know, and the fact that he did know was certainly not common knowledge. Slade wondered if he told his ill-fated *amigo* how to get there. If he did, and it was discovered by somebody desirous of keeping the location a secret, that could be the explanation of why he was killed. But why was somebody so anxious that the spot not be visited? Again the question that intrigued El Halcon not a little.

Relative to one angle, Slade had a definite hunch that in some manner the Diamond H would be the focal point of any development relative to the matter. Just why he felt that way he couldn't explain, but he did, and he had learned to be chary of disregarding hunches, which, he knew, were often but the outcome of marshalling known facts that refused to be accurately catalogued but which in a murky way formed a definite pattern he eventually would be able to understand.

Slade knew his chief handicap at the moment was due to the fact that he had not the least notion who to look for. However he had been in the section only a couple of days so that was not remarkable. So far he had met only a few of the more prominent people of the community, including Arn Harvey, Miles Pacer, Border Shift Brewster, Steve Gore and a few others with whom he had spoken casually. He hoped to remedy the situation before long. And he was getting some notion of the relation of the various localities one to another.

He thought about the individuals he could be said to have really contacted. Outstanding, he felt, was Steve Gore, although perhaps it was only his picturesque attire that caused him to stand out a bit. Steve Gore did interest him, and not altogether because of the way he dressed. Gore showed indications of being an able man and a hard man; but Mississippi River gamblers were usually both. Also, Slade did not overlook the quite apparent fact that his neighbors regarded him a bit askance. His hiring Mexican *vaqueros* and Yaquis for cowhands explained that to an extent, of course. And he was a comparative newcomer in the section. Miles Pacer was also a newcomer, having taken over the Booger F not long after Gore's arrival, but the fact that his father before him had been an inhabitant of the section gave him a certain status of permanency that Gore did not enjoy.

A few minutes later the very man of whom he had been thinking came in, nodded cordially and passed to the bar, where he was soon engaged in conversation with Border Shift Brewster.

Steve Gore was, as usual, immaculately dressed and Slade thought he looked even more the part of the steamboat gambler than he had the previous night. His manner was assured, his bearing could be almost called debonaire. He appeared more the sophisticated man of the world than the Texas cattleman, aside from his deeply bronzed skin which bespoke much outdoor living.

Slade noted Gore slant a glance in his direction. He surmised that Border Shift was regaling Gore with an account of his morning's adventure. That he was correct in his conjecture was proven shortly afterward when Gore placed his empty glass on the bar and sauntered over to the table.

"Congratulations!" he said. "Border Shift told me all about it. Seems you're better than holding your own with the scum. Mind if I sit down?"

"It'll be a pleasure," Slade returned. Gore nodded and drew up a chair.

"Had to come in to arrange for some stock cars," he announced. "Hope to get a shipping herd together for next week. Have you tied onto anything yet?"

"Arn Harvey offered me a job with the Diamond H," Slade replied.

"I think you'll do well to take it," Gore said. "I've seen him a couple of times and like his looks. I gather he's a smart rancher, and he impressed me as being a square man."

"Yes, I think he's both," Slade agreed.

"Most of the old-timers in this section are, I'd say," Gore added. "They mostly look sort of sideways at me, but I don't mind. They'll get over it after a while."

He was silent a moment, eyeing Slade speculatively. "How'd you like to amble down and look my place over?" he suggested. "Only a few hours' ride. We'll have a good dinner and I'll put you up for the night. I'd like to show you what I've done with the holding; I'm rather proud of what I've accomplished in a year."

Slade hesitated an instant but decided to accept the invitation. He was curious about Gore and no matter what the Bradded L owner was or wasn't, he didn't consider there was much risk involved. It would be a bit too obvious, with them riding out of town together and a hundred pairs of eyes noting the fact.

"Reckon I could do worse," he replied. "Nothing pressing to do this afternoon and the inquest won't be held till tomorrow. I'm ready whenever you are."

They left Sanders by way of the trail by which Slade rode from the Diamond H ranchhouse, but a mile out of town Gore turned into a fork that diagonalled from the main trail in a southwesterly direction. As they followed it the country changed some-what till it was in the form of a fairly wide valley with long slopes, thickly grown with chaparral, rolling upward to a rounded skyline. Another half hour and they began passing clumps of cattle bearing the Bradded L burn. Slade noted that they were just about the best looking cows he had yet observed in the section.

"Yes, I'm going in for improved stock," Gore replied to his comment. "The long-horn market is failing and we might as well admit it. People are demanding better meat than the old mossyback can provide and ranchers who don't take that obvious fact into consideration are going to have trouble disposing of their product. I decided to get the jump on the market rather than franti-cally endeavoring to catch up with it later."

Soon Slade noted something else. Scat-tered about were little tin windmills indus-triously pumping water for the waterholes, each of which provided its own little trickle that leavened an area of range.

"I got this holding cheap," Gore observed. "I decided it was good range except for one thing; it was a dry pasture. But the whole terrain is in the nature of a wide and shal-low trough. I figured that an indication of an underground water supply, so I drilled a few wells and proved I was right. I'm getting plenty of water, now. I'm putting down more wells and placing more windmills as fast as I can afford it. Another year or so and I figure to have a first class spread."

Slade nodded agreement. His estimate of Steve Gore as a cattleman had risen.

The trail wound along the base of the southwestern slope which rolled gently upward for better than a third of a mile and was heavily brush grown. While he spoke with Gore, Slade's glance was constantly roving over the silent sag. His eyes narrowed a little as he was pretty sure he sensed movement some six hundred yards above where they rode. A moment later and he was without a doubt. Not only had he noted a drifting shadow along a more sparsely grown stretch, but he had caught a quick gleam as of sunlight reflecting on metal. His hand instinctively dropped toward the butt of the Winchester snugged in the saddle boot. Steve Gore noticed the gesture.

"Spotted him, eh?" he remarked. "You must have eyes that can see through a side of hill. I know he's up there but I can't see a sign of him."

"Who is it?" Slade asked, flickering a sideways glance at the rancher and at the same time keeping the shadowy slope under surveillance.

"One of my Yaquis," Gore replied. "They're the reason why I've lost less cows than anybody else in the section. I have three of them and they spend most of their time riding around in the hills and keeping under cover, that is from the average eyesight. Four times in the past six months they've spotted gents taking an undue interest in one of my herds. I immediately posted triple guards and had no trouble. The hellions, whoever they were, saw I was prepared for them and laid off."

Slade nodded his understanding. Gore's expedient was simple but ingenious. There were no better brush riders than Yaquis and they could pretty well be depended on to spot anything off-color; then when Gore increased his guard force he served notice that he was anticipating a raid and was ready for it. That alone would be enough to cause the rustlers to refrain from an attempt on his stock. Success in cow stealing, whether the running off of a herd or the filching of individual animals, was largely dependent on catching the owner unawares. And no larcenous bunch hankers for a pitched battle with a prepared outfit.

Studying the contours of the holding, Slade also deduced that the terrain was not admirably adapted to widelooping activities despite the proximity of the Rio Grande. Doubtless the only convenient exit from the shallow trough was by way of its southwest mouth, which narrowed the potentialities. Cattle could negotiate the slopes, all right, but their progress would be slow and with plenty of plain evidence of their passing. With the Diamond H and the Booger F the situation was reversed. Raiders could turn in any direction to thorny pastures and hidden trails with which they were doubtless familiar.

Another hour of riding and they sighted an old ranchhouse set in a grove of ancient oaks. It showed signs of recent rebuilding and repair.

"She was a shack when I took her over," said Gore. "Now I've got a comfortable home."

Bunkhouse, corrals and other outbuildings were tight and well cared for. There was no doubt but Steve Gore was a conscientious and progressive owner. And everything pointed to intentions of permanent residence. Slade remarked on the fact.

"Yes, I'm here to stay," Gore replied. "I was brought up on a ranch and after sashaying around for quite a spell I decided that on a ranch was where I belonged. So, having saved a small hunk of *dinero,* I began looking around for something suitable that was within my means. This holding appeared to have everything I wanted so I bought it and went to work on it."

"And there's no doubt but what you've done a splendid job," Slade conceded.

"Yes, I'm pleased with what I've accomplished," Gore said, adding with a touch of bitterness, "and if I can only finally persuade my neighbors not to look sideways at me I'll be content."

"I think you will succeed in that, perhaps sooner than you anticipate," Slade remarked.

"I hope so," Gore answered. "Well, unfork and we'll amble in; chuck should be on the table before long. I've got a good cook. You can't beat Mexicans for that chore."

"And there are no better cowhands, once you persuade them that there's more to ranch work than fancy riding and roping," Slade commented. Gore cast him a curious glance.

"I gather you don't hold anything against Mexicans because they are Mexicans," he observed.

Slade suddenly let the full force of his level gray eyes rest on the ranchowner's face. "Mr. Gore," he said, "I do not hold anything against anybody who is square and decent. Mexicans are people, just as we are, and," he added, "so are Yaqui Indians. I've found that people largely fall into two categories: they're good or they're bad, and the color of their skins, their nationalities or their beliefs have little to do with the matter."

"My sentiments," Gore agreed soberly. "Let's go eat."

TWELVE

When Slade entered the dining room where the hands were already assembled, he was instantly the focus of all eyes. He moved his head in a barely perceptible negative gesture; the *vaqueros* immediately dropped their gaze to their plates and went on talking and eating as if nothing out of the ordinary had happened. Slade spoke with them in Spanish and even, to the evident delight of the dark-faced Yaquis, managed to drop a few words in their own mountain dialect. Indians, contrary to popular belief, are not always taciturn or devoid of a sense of humor. The Yaquis chattered as volubly as anybody else and their white teeth flashed in frequent grins.

The meal was excellent, the atmosphere cheerful and pleasant. It was plain to see

131

that the Mexican and Yaqui cowboys not only respected their employer but had a genuine affection for him. Slade felt that their loyalty was unquestioned. And gradually he formed the opinion that these pleasant, well-spoken young men were honest to the core. Which, while satisfying on general principles, certainly did not help with the problem that confronted him as a Texas Ranger.

After they finished eating, Slade and Gore repaired to the living room where they discussed range matters at length. Gore, who seemed glad to have someone to talk to, asked many questions relative to the cattle business in other parts of the state and outlined his long range plans, all of which Slade thought commendable. Finally, however, the ranchowner fell silent and sat regarding his guest and apparently turning something over in his mind.

"I couldn't help but notice the curious effect you had on my men," he said abruptly. "They accorded you a deference, almost reverence, one would expect them to reserve for a bishop of their faith. Slade, do you always have that effect on strangers?"

Slade chuckled, the lights of laughter dancing in his gray eyes, but did not otherwise reply. Gore evidently decided that further questions would be out of order and would doubtless not be answered. At any rate he changed the subject and queried Slade as to the, in his opinion, advisability of growing alfalfa for winter forage.

Slade rode to Sanders early the following morning. He rode with less regard than usual for his surroundings, for he knew very well that up on the slopes three dark-faced riders were pacing him and that he had little to worry about. He had enjoyed his visit with Steve Gore, but had to confess, a bit wryly, that the results had been noticeable for their absence. His most promising suspect had virtually eliminated himself. For unless he was making a thundering mistake, and he didn't think he was, there was nothing off-color about Steve Gore.

Now where was he to turn? Slade hadn't the slightest notion. He could only await developments. Reaching Sanders, he stabled his horse and hunted up Sheriff Bascomb.

The inquest was briefer even than the former one. The verdict allowed that the two sidewinders got exactly what was coming to them and recommended that Slade keep up the good work, with an added somewhat caustic recommendation that Sheriff Bascomb warm his chair less and stir his stumps more.

Although the hour was early, Sanders was already growing a bit lively, for it was pay day for the neighboring spreads. Rows of ponies stood at the convenient hitchracks and their riders were thronging the saloons and other places of entertainment. Slade gathered that quite a few folks from the oil fields always came over to join in the celebration. Which tended to make things even more hilarious.

"Usually doesn't amount to much beside a few broken heads and run-of-mine rukuses," said Sheriff Bascomb. "I got a few special deputies circulating around to cool 'em down if they get obstreperous."

Slade repaired to the Widow Maker for a drink and a bite to eat. When he entered he saw Miles Pacer sitting at a table. The Booger F owner beckoned him to come over and called to a waiter to bring drinks.

"Understand things are still moving for you," he observed as Slade sat down. "Glad to see you came out of the latest with a whole skin. It would appear you've made some bad enemies in a hurry."

"Looks sort of that way," Slade conceded noncommittally.

"I imagine they'll leave you alone after their latest failure," Pacer predicted.

"Wouldn't be surprised if they've got a belly-ful."

"Possibly," Slade agreed. Personally, he did not think so.

After discussing their drink they sat smoking and watching the dancers on the crowded floor. A tall, dark girl with flashing black eyes and red lips swayed up to the table and voiced a question in liquid Spanish.

Pacer hesitated and, involuntarily, it seemed to Slade, cast him a questioning look.

"I've a notion she's asking us if we want to dance," Slade said.

"Reckon that's it," Pacer agreed.

"I'll find out," Slade said. He gestured inquiringly to the dance floor. The girl smiled and nodded.

"Reckon I might as well give it a whirl," Slade said to Pacer. He rose, smiled at the girl and followed her across the room. As they circled the dance floor, she murmured softly in Spanish, "And why does El Halcon pretend not to understand?"

"There are reasons, *Señorita*," Slade replied briefly in the same tongue.

"*Sí?*" the girl whispered. "If El Halcon has reasons, that is enough for Teresa. From now we speak only in *Ingles*, which I speak but badly."

"And there goes the finest looking couple I ever saw or ever expect to see," remarked a grizzled old cowboy at a nearby poker table, staring enviously at the tall, lithe Hawk and forgetting the full house he held.

And it was this particular moment that Arn Harvey and his daughter chose to enter the Widow Maker.

Harvey instantly spotted Slade and bellowed a greeting. Audrey favored him with a very cool look and spoke to Miles Pacer.

Teresa, whose sharp eyes had noted this bit of byplay, giggled delightedly as the music stopped. "Go join your *amigos,*" she whispered. "The little *muchacha* she is beautiful."

With another giggle she slipped from his embrace and scampered to a table on the far side of the floor, where a handsome young *vaquero* welcomed her with a wide grin.

"Take a load off your feet, son," old Arn invited as Slade sauntered back to his own table. "Sit down and keep Audrey company. I'm ambling down to the general store to attend to a few chores and Miles is going with me. We'll be back in fifteen or twenty minutes and we'll all eat."

He clumped out, Pacer following. Audrey

looked Slade up and down.

"Well, you see it was like this —" Slade began.

"Oh, don't bother to explain," she interrupted. "A woman never pays any attention to a man's explanations, anyhow."

Slade was about to return a bantering reply when he realized there was real trouble in the big eyes.

"Honey, you're not taking it seriously?" he protested.

"Of course not," she answered impatiently, "but Walt, I'm scared, and I mean badly scared. We heard about what happened on the trail yesterday morning. Why is somebody so anxious to kill you?"

"Audrey, I don't know," he admitted frankly, "but they're not having much luck, so don't worry your pretty head about it."

"But I am worried, I can't help it," she answered.

Slade chuckled. "Would you like to dance?" he suggested as the orchestra began a dreamy Spanish waltz.

"I'd love to," she replied.

As they passed his table, the old poker player who had commented earlier remarked, "I said I never expected to see a finer looking couple, but I am. That one is purtier than the other one, and she dances better. Some jiggers have all the luck!"

Audrey was a good dancer, but Slade had trouble keeping his mind on his charming partner. He was still trying to analyze the surprising discovery he had made a short time before, when Teresa approached the table and voiced her simple question.

Miles Pacer did not understand Spanish!

THIRTEEN

After the dance, Slade and Audrey went back to their table. Border Shift Brewster came over with a word of greeting.

"Seems everybody's in town today," he remarked. "They brought in another big oil well over on the Ray ranch yesterday and all the boys are dropping in to talk about it. Appears everybody is going loco about oil. Reckon it won't be long till cattle raising is a thing of the past."

Slade smilingly shook his head. "There'll be cattle raising in this section so long as there are prickly pear and dagger, and I figure that will be a long time," he said. "The oil discoveries, just like the railroad, will bring in a lot of new people, and that's good for the cattle business. Those folks will have to eat and it's up to the cowmen to grow the beef. What it will do is prosper the cow business. Besides, a cowman is a cow-man and always will be. No matter what he turns his hand to, he's got too much horse and grass rope in his blood to ever really be anything else. He'll always find an excuse to raise cattle."

"Wouldn't be surprised if you have the right notion," Border Shift agreed. "Let's have a drink on it."

Arn Harvey returned shortly afterward, alone. "Miles had some chores of his own to look after," he explained. "Maybe he'll join us later. Let's eat."

He proceeded to order everything on the bill of fare.

"Got news," he announced after he had finished with the waiter. "They didn't bring in one new well on the Ray holdings, they brought in two, and both gushers. Things are jumpin' over there. Guess old George Ray is sort of beside himself. Anyhow, he declared a holiday for tomorrow — would have done it today, but they had to get the wells capped. He's handing every man a nice fat bonus so they can really celebrate. This town will hum tomorrow. Nothing over there at the fields but a railroad flag stop and a rumhole or two; they'll be coming here for the bust."

After his hunger was assuaged, old Arn

stuffed his pipe with tobacco and twinkled his eyes at Slade.

"Suppose you'll be staying in a while for the pay day bust, son," he remarked. "Okay, the boys will all be here and you can ride home with them. Don't reckon the gents who are gunning for you will care to tackle the whole bunch. All right with you?"

"That'll be fine," Slade replied, with a glance at Audrey, who looked decidedly relieved.

Harvey finished his smoke and had another drink. He glanced at the clock over the bar.

"Reckon Miles ain't coming back," he observed. "He said he had a lot to look after and might decide to go home. Guess that's what he did.

"Well, come on, chick," he said to Audrey. "Time we were going home, too."

Shortly afterward the Diamond H bunch rolled in, wizened, cantankerous old Si Cooley, the range boss, heading the pack. They greeted Slade uproariously and insisted he have a drink with them.

After emptying his glass, Slade went back to the kitchen to see Sancho Rojas.

"I am content here, and here I feel safe," the old Mexican said.

"I think you are," Slade agreed. "Maybe

after a bit things will clear up, but right now here's where you belong. Stick around close."

As dusk fell the Widow Maker grew progressively livelier. Hands from the farther spreads were streaming into town and the evening train brought a contingent of workers from the oil field. Slade watched the hilarity a while, with enjoyment, and then strolled about the streets. Around midnight he stopped at the sheriff's office.

"Everything peaceful," said Bascomb. "Nothing but the usual wrangling and disagreements; nothing serious."

Right at that moment things were also peaceful at the oil field fifteen miles to the east, but not for long. In the office the paymaster and his two clerks were busy making up the promised bonus. Stacks of envelopes lay on the paymaster's desk, in which the allotment to each worker was placed and carefully checked. Stacks of bills and rolls of gold pieces were counted and parcelled. Outside an alert watchman patrolled. There were other watchmen scattered about, keeping an eye on the derricks and the pumping machinery.

The watchman sauntered around a corner of the building, swinging his lantern. He turned at a slight sound behind him, the last sound he was to hear for some time. A gun barrel crashed against his skull and he slumped to the ground, the lantern falling from his nerveless hand. His attacker scooped it up before it flickered out. Three more men materialized from the shadows. They glided along the building and flattened themselves against the wall near the door. The fourth man circled around and approached the lighted window. He called something unintelligible and waved the lantern.

Inside the office one of the clerks looked up. "Old Arnold, the watchman, wants something," he said. "He's waving his lantern and yelling; here he comes to the door."

"Open it and let him in," grunted the paymaster, busy with his figures.

The clerk rose, stretched his cramped limbs and walked to the door. He unlocked it and swung it open, and looked squarely into a gun muzzle. Behind the gun was a man wearing a black mask. Back of him crowded three more masked men.

The paymaster turned at the commotion and made the mistake of grabbing for a gun that lay in an open drawer. The leading bandit shot him through the head. Another knocked the clerk unconscious with a gun barrel. The three crowded into the room, their guns menacing the remaining clerk who cowered behind the table, his mouth forming the O of a soundless scream, his eyes bulging with terror.

While one man held a gun on the clerk, his two companions scooped up money and envelopes and thrust them into a sack. In less than a minute they had cleared the table. They grabbed what was in the open safe and hurried out the door, closing it behind them.

Outside shouted questions sounded; lanterns bobbed as the other watchmen who had heard the shot converged on the office building. The bandits raced across an open space toward a grove a hundred paces or so from the building. One of the watchmen, quicker witted than his fellows, began shooting at the flitting figures. An answering volley sent him and the others diving for cover. The bandits vanished into the grove. Another moment and they crashed out on the far side, heading for the dark loom of the hills less than a mile to the west. The watchmen and others aroused by the tumult gave chase, shouting and shooting, but were soon outdistanced. Giving up the pursuit they hurried back to the office to find the dead paymaster and the unconscious clerk. The second clerk, gibbering with fright, managed to tell them what had happened. The whole field boiled with activity, but it was not until George Ray himself appeared that anybody thought to run to the railroad station and telegraph for the sheriff.

One of Sheriff Bascomb's deputies had just entered and Slade was preparing to leave when a man rushed in shouting and waving a yellow sheet of paper. It was the railroad telegraph operator.

"Robbers!" he babbled. "Over to the oil field. Killed the paymaster! Sheriff, they want you at once!"

Sheriff Bascomb, whose nerves were not easily discomposed, rose to his feet. "Take it easy," he said. "What else did they tell you?"

"That's all I could get," replied the operator, calming down a bit. "Some ham was working the key; I could hardly make out what he was sending."

The sheriff turned to the deputy. "Go get the boys," he ordered. "Two or three should do."

He turned to Slade as the deputy hurried out. "Suppose you'll want to go along," he observed. "Never mind getting sworn in. You're packing all the authority you need, or I'm a heap mistaken. Oh, I haven't been peace officering for twenty years for nothing. How'd you leave Jim McNelty? I used to know him."

"He was fine," Slade replied with a smile. "Keep it under your hat for a while, please."

"I'm not in the habit of shooting off my mouth," grunted the sheriff. "Come on, let's get our horses. Pete should have the boys rounded up soon."

Word of the outrage had spread like wildfire and a crowd was gathered in the street when they emerged from the office. Slade spotted Si Cooley, the Diamond H range boss, and drew him aside.

"When you get back to the ranch, tell Mr. Harvey or Miss Audrey that I'm riding with the sheriff, and that I'll try and make it to the place sometime tomorrow," he told Cooley.

"Okay," the range boss agreed. "We'll be heading for the spread before long. This hullabaloo has sobered everybody up."

Twenty minutes later the posse, six strong, rode out of Sanders on the east-west trail that for a portion of the distance paralleled the railroad.

The oil field was still undergoing considerable turmoil when they arrived there after two hours of hard riding. They found old

George Ray pacing the office in a towering rage.

"I don't give a darn about the money, although it was better'n ten thousand dollars, but they killed poor Adams," he said. "Oh, it was those infernal Dawn Riders, all right. They wore black masks and nobody else would have the nerve to pull a thing like that. Well, the boys won't have their celebration today, but they'll have it next week, on pay day. I've already wired for more money. I hope you'll have a nice necktie party for us to liven things up, Bascomb."

"Got to catch your rabbit 'fore you cook it," grunted the sheriff. "Did anybody see which way they went?"

"Some of the boys followed them a piece and saw them go into that canyon over to the west," Ray replied.

"They'll have to keep going till they reach the other end, there's no turning aside in that crack," observed the sheriff. "It'll be getting light in another hour, so I reckon we might as well be riding. What do you think, Slade?"

"I think we'd better wait until it is getting light," Slade replied. "They've got a long head start and we can't hope to overtake them; our only hope is to track them down, and we need daylight for that. Besides, although I doubt if it's likely, I wouldn't put it past a bunch like that to hole up in the canyon and wait for somebody to come along."

"You're right about that," agreed the sheriff. "Would be just like the sidewinders; we'll wait till daylight. George, see if you can round up some coffee and a sandwich or two while we're waiting. I'm hungry and the devil knows when we'll get another chance to eat."

By the time the coffee was drunk the east was brightening with morning. Slade glanced out the window. "Guess we can risk it now," he said. "That canyon faces east and the sun will get into it early."

The first rays of the rising sun had banished the gloom when they entered the gorge. Slade quickly saw that horses had passed that way recently. Sheriff Bascomb declared there was no place where a band of horsemen could turn aside so they rode at a good pace, Slade nevertheless keeping an eye on the trail. But when they left the west mouth of the canyon the tracks still led on ahead. Followed stony ground and thorny pastures, the keen eyes of El Halcon missed nothing. An overturned boulder, a dangling twig or a branch stripped of some of its leaves was enough to keep him on the right track.

As they covered mile after mile, Sheriff Bascomb's spirits rose. "At this rate we'll get 'em," he declared. "The way you spot things they'll never be able to give us the slip. I reckon the hellions didn't count on you."

Slade, however, was not inclined to be so optimistic. "There's something funny about this," he said. "To all appearances they are not making the slightest attempt to cover their trail. Looks like they know they'll be able to give us the slip when they're ready to. Well, all we can do is keep on going."

More miles were covered, always in a westerly direction, then abruptly the tracks turned almost due south. Slade's black brows drew together, but he did not comment. Another half hour and they topped a long ridge with the far sag dropping steeply downward. Slade pulled up, the others jostling to a halt behind him.

"Foiled! as the villain said in the play," he remarked, apparently with no surprise.

"What do you mean?" asked the sheriff.

"I mean," Slade replied, "that we've been nicely outsmarted. Here is where they took the east-west trail. See it down there at the bottom of the slope? That trail isn't used as much as it was before the railroad came along, but it's still used enough to make identifying any particular set of tracks impossible."

"But that trail runs right to town," the sheriff protested.

"Naturally, that's why they took it," Slade replied. "They rode right into town, hitched their horses at the racks along with a hundred others and mingled with the crowd. Absolutely in the clear and with alibis provided if they should happen to need them, which they won't. Been right in town all evening and ready to prove it. Busy bartenders would remember serving them but would be vague as to time. A shrewd bunch, all right, plenty of wrinkles on their horns. Yes, we were nicely outsmarted. While we were sifting sand east along that trail down there, they were riding parallel to us through the hills, but headed west, and doubtless snickering over how they'd put it across. A bunch with savvy."

Sheriff Bascomb swore till the air smelled of sulphur. His deputies tried to keep up with him and failed. Slade rolled a cigarette and smoked calmly until the storm had subsided somewhat.

"Guess we'd better amble on to town," he suggested. "Very likely we'll be taking a drink at the same bar with one or more of them, and they'll be grinning inside."

That started the sheriff off again. "Oh, blasted, what's the use!" he broke off. "The hellions did it again, that's all. Why did I ever quit following a cow's tail! Monotonous but easier on the disposition. Let's go!"

The discomfited posse arrived in Sanders an hour later. Slade made sure Shadow had everything he needed and then repaired to the Widow Maker for a late breakfast. When he entered the saloon a curious sight met his eyes. Sprawled in chairs, in various states of drowse, were Si Cooley and four of the Diamond H cowboys. Cooley waved a somnolent hand.

"What the devil are you jiggers doing here this time of the morning?" Slade asked.

"Waiting for you," Cooley replied non-committally.

"W-waiting for me!" Slade sputtered. "Why? I thought you were heading back to the ranch right after midnight."

"Oh, we did," Cooley returned. "When we got there Miss Audrey was sittin' up in the living room. I told her what you told me to tell her and she filled us up with coffee and sent us right back here to make sure you got home okay."

"Good Lord!" Slade exploded. "There

was no sense in that."

"Maybe," Cooley agreed, "but I don't argue with no females. Especially not with Miss Audrey who's been practically running that shebang for the past three or four years; it ain't safe."

"Okay," Slade said resignedly. "I'll grab a bite to eat and then we'll ride."

"Take your time, we're comfortable," Cooley answered. "And Slade," he added, his voice suddenly serious, "everything considered, I figure Miss Audrey did right."

While Slade was eating, Miles Pacer came in. His eyes were red-rimmed and he looked tired, but was smiling as usual.

"No luck, eh?" he remarked as he paused at Slade's table. "I would like to have gone with you fellows but I heard about it too late."

"Been in town all night?" Slade asked.

"Most of it," Pacer replied. "I got back from my spread about ten o'clock and stopped at a couple of places down the street. Got into a poker game later. Now I'm going home to bed soon as I get a drink."

With a pleasant nod he passed to the bar, downed a glass of whiskey and walked out. Slade contemplated his broad back as he passed through the swinging doors and his eyes were thoughtful.

Old Arn was out on the range but Audrey was still up when Slade arrived at the Diamond H ranchhouse in company with the weary punchers. Her eyes were heavy from lack of sleep but they brightened as he entered the room.

"I hope you're not put out over what I did," she said. "I figured you wouldn't be exactly yourself when you started home and I didn't see any sense of your taking needless chances."

"You could have been right," he admitted.

FOURTEEN

"Well, son, are you going to sign up with us?" old Arn asked that evening as they sat in the living room after supper.

"Yes, I think I will," Slade replied. "Appears to be a nice holding you've got."

"I'll have to play square and admit it ain't when it comes to working it," Harvey chuckled. "After a sashay through the *granjeno* you ain't got much hide left on you and you're lucky if you still got your pants, but I got a string of good brush horses and I reckon a prickly chore won't bother a gent like you much. As Border Shift says, let's have a drink on it."

Slade went to work for the Diamond H. Cooley, the range boss, who recognized a tophand when he saw one, merely told him what he wanted done and left him to his own devices, which suited Slade admirably. It gave him plenty of opportunity to look over the country and do some explorative riding in the hills. And while he worked with his hands his mind was busy. He had plenty to think about, including the utterly puzzling fact that Miles Pacer didn't understand Spanish. Slade was formulating a vague theory relative to Miles Pacer, a theory that on the face of it appeared preposterous. In fact, Slade himself wondered if he wasn't figuratively chasing after moonbeams. But the theory was in the nature of a hunch and refused to be downed.

Several times in the course of his riding he encountered one or more of the Booger F cowhands. They were pleasant, well-spoken young fellows, mostly local boys who, Slade gathered, had been born and brought up in the section. He certainly gleaned nothing of value from them. At times his thoughts would go back to Steve Gore and now and then he experienced a subtle uneasiness over his estimate of the Bradded L owner. If he'd made a mistake in judging Steve Gore he was likely to pay for it, unpleasantly.

Slade quickly realized that Arn Harvey hadn't exaggerated when he said the range was a tough one to work. The cattle were among the wildest Slade had ever encountered. Often he could hear *ladino* cows popping the bushes half a mile away, with not a horn in sight. Combing out strays from the brakes of prickly pear and dagger was a hefty chore.

But Arn Harvey had plenty of good brush horses and Slade, who had worked similar range before and, after all, had been born a cattleman, really enjoyed it. However, he did not particularly enjoy the experience he had about a week after signing with Harvey.

He was riding a broken section well to the north and near where Miles Pacer's Booger F joined with the Diamond H. It was a lonely and deserted terrain slashed with gorges and canyons where fat beefs holed up to escape the heat. Slade was making a tally of possible shipping prospects. Atop a low but steep sag he pulled up to allow the chunky bay he was riding a breathing spell. As usual, his eyes constantly scanned the surrounding country.

Abruptly his gaze fixed; he had sensed movement in the mouth of a dark gorge some hundreds of yards to the south. A moment later the movement materialized into four horsemen riding out of the canyon. Slade's hand tightened on the bridle as he watched them head purposefully for the slope; his eye caught a flash of metal. He whirled the bay on a dime and sent him charging down the opposite sag. Over his head a bullet whined. The crack of a rifle slammed the echoes back and forth.

"Thought so," he muttered. Mechanically his hand dropped to where his Winchester should have snugged in the saddle boot beneath his left thigh. Then he swore in exasperation. The bay, a much smaller horse than Shadow, could not handle the big black's ponderous saddle and the light rig he bore was not equipped with a boot. The long gun was in the Diamond H ranch-house. Just one of those oversights committed by the most careful at times.

"Sixes against rifles. Not so good," he told the bay. "Feller, I reckon it's up to you. Sift sand, jughead, those hellions back there don't want to just play tag with us; they're playing for keeps."

The small horse was giving his best, but Slade quickly realized it wasn't enough. The pursuers were undoubtedly better mounted and their animals were fresh, while the bay had already had a hard day of slugging through the brush. Before he reached the bottom of the slope the pursuit had topped the rise and the bullets they kept sending after him were coming uncomfortably close.

On the level ground at the foot of the sag the bay held his own, even gained a little while the pursuers were negotiating the rocky slope; but once they reached the level it was a different story. Slowly, but surely they were drawing nearer. Slade settled himself in the saddle and proceeded to get everything possible out of his mount. The shooting had stopped but he derived no comfort from the fact. It was plain that the four horsemen realized he didn't have a rifle and were endeavoring to cut his lead to just beyond pistol range. Then they would open fire again with greater accuracy. He loosened his big Colts in their sheaths although he had little hope of getting a chance to use them, the way things were going. Once the pursuers started shooting it was just a matter of time till a lucky shot dropped him. It began to look very much like curtains; he'd overplayed his hand and got caught with a bobtailed flush against four of a kind.

Despite the seriousness of the situation, he chuckled at the thought; his horse did have a short tail and there were four of a kind, all right, steadily closing the distance.

But the bay had caught his second wind and was giving a good account of himself. On and on he scudded, blowing and snorting, his nostrils flaring red, his eyes rolling. Slade began experiencing a thrill of hope and was almost prepared to abandon the desperate plan of whirling suddenly and charging back on the chance of getting close enough to put his sixes into action before he was dropped. Only a mile or two farther was the old east-west trail, along which at this time of day there was often considerable traffic.

But the bay was beginning to falter. He had given all he had to give. Slade's hand tightened on the bridle. Then abruptly he saw a flash of light ahead. A moment later he realized it was a gleam of late sunlight reflecting from the twin steel ribbons of the railroad only a hundred yards ahead. And booming out of the west was a long freight train. But he could never make it across the tracks in time. He was blocked!

Behind him the pursuers whooped in triumph and began shooting, the slugs whistling close. But abruptly Slade's eyes blazed with exultation. What had looked like his finish might be his salvation. He sent the bay charging forward as the locomotive roared past, pluming black smoke. The right-of-way was less than fifty yards distant. The long line of boxcars was rocking over the rails at high speed.

Slade veered the bay to the left and sent him scudding along parallel to the speeding train. Carefully he edged him nearer and nearer the tie ends. He stood in his stirrups, gauged the distance and, leaning far over, gripped a grabiron on the side of a passing car.

He was jerked from the saddle with a force that almost loosened his arms in the shoulder sockets, but he grimly held on, dangling and banging against the side of the car. One hand was torn loose from its hold but he managed to retain his grip with the other. With a mighty effort he drew himself up until he could grasp the grabiron above with his free hand. Then he flung his body sideways, caught the end grabirons and hurled himself in between the cars. Above the roar of the train he heard the howls of rage of the frustrated pursuers and a banging of rifles. Bullets spatted against the sides of the cars, glanced off the grabirons, clanged against the spinning wheels; but he was crouched on the end-sill of the forward car and out of sight. He had a last glimpse of the bay horse careening off through the brush in the direction of home. Then the train whisked around a curve and the shooting and yelling ceased. Slade straightened up to ease his cramped muscles.

"Well," he chuckled as the freight train roared on towards Sanders, "that was plain bull luck and nothing else. Got dealt the joker on the last round!"

The freight train stopped at Sanders for water. Slade slipped from his perch without attracting attention. He hurried to the livery stable, hired a horse and set out for the Diamond H ranchhouse. He hoped to arrive there ahead of the homing bay with his empty saddle, but he didn't quite make it.

He found Arn Harvey badly worried and Audrey in a state bordering on hysteria.

"My God, son!" exclaimed the rancher. "I figured they'd got you this time for sure. What the devil happened?"

Slade told him. Harvey swore in anger and exasperation. "Never in my born days did I hear tell of such a persistent bunch of pestiferous hellions," he declared. "Ain't they ever going to give up?"

"Well, as I said before," Slade smiled, "they're not having much luck."

Old Arn wagged his head dubiously. Audrey dropped into a chair and covered her eyes with her hand. Her father gazed at her and clucked sympathetically.

"Don't ever marry a cowhand, honey, if you don't want to go plumb loco," he advised.

"It wouldn't be so bad if he was just a cowhand," she burst out.

Old Arn stared at her. "Now what do you mean by that?" he demanded.

Audrey was silent. Slade arrived at a decision.

"She caught on and so did Sheriff Bascomb, so I reckon there's no reason to hold out on you, sir," he said. He slipped something from a cunningly concealed secret pocket in his broad leather belt and passed it to the rancher.

Old Arn stared at the famous silver star set on a silver circle, the feared and honored badge of the Texas Rangers!

"Well, I'll — I'll be darned!" he sputtered. "You're a Ranger! I might have known it, though; nobody but a Ranger could have done the things you have since you've been here."

"Captain McNelty got your letter, among others," Slade explained. "He figured I'd better ride down and look things over. You used to know McNelty, did you not?"

"Sure I used to know him," replied Harvey. "I've had many a drink with him. Fine feller. And now something's beginning to click! Walt Slade! I thought that name had a familiar ring, but there are lots of Slades in Texas and I didn't give it any thought. Aren't you the Ranger the Mexicans call El Halcon?"

"I've been called that," Slade admitted with a smile.

Old Arn stared, almost in awe, at the man whose exploits were legend throughout the Southwest. "If this don't take the shingles off the barn!" he exclaimed. "El Halcon! And you're working for me," he added with a chuckle.

"Yes, it gives me a good excuse for hanging around the section," Slade replied. He did not add that if the vague theory he was struggling with was substantial, the Diamond H would be concerned in whatever developed.

"Been getting any results, aside from thinning out the sidewinders?" Harvey asked.

"Well," Slade answered a bit wryly, "so far about all I've done is dodge lead and run around in circles, but maybe things will break, sooner or later."

"They will," old Arn declared positively. "Rather, you'll make 'em break."

"If he manages to stay alive that long," Audrey put in dolefully.

"Don't worry about him, honey," chuckled

her father. "That's what they call him —
the Ranger who can't be killed. Did you get
a look at those devils who chased you
today?" he asked.

"They never got closer than about four
hundred yards, fortunately for me," Slade
replied. "And at that distance faces are just
a blur."

"They weren't masked, then?"

Slade shook his head. "I guess they figured
they wouldn't need any, that even if I did
get a look at them I wouldn't be mentioning it to anybody. Looked for a while like
they had it figured right."

Harvey nodded and was silent for a few
minutes while Slade smoked. Then he announced, "I'm riding to town tomorrow
afternoon with the boys. George Ray finally
got things straightened out at the oil fields
and is handing his men their bonus. Tomorrow's pay day at the fields, too, so things
should be sort of lively in Sanders tomorrow. Don't you think it would be a good
notion to come along with us?"

"Yes, I think it would," Slade agreed.

"And you'll be safer riding in with us,"
Harvey nodded. "I don't think any aggrega-
tion of hellions would care to tackle the
whole Diamond H outfit. Fact is, I wish
they would; we'd save you some bother.

Okay, don't go out on the range in the morning. Stick around the house and we'll ride after dinner."

FIFTEEN

They rode to town the next day as planned, but did not get started until considerably later than was expected, arriving at Sanders just about sunset. They found the town crowded with the celebrating oil workers, and cowhands from the various spreads who had ridden in to take part in the fun. It was a gay and turbulent crowd but, to all appearances at least, a harmless gathering. Sheriff Bascomb took no chances, however, and had special deputies on the job.

Slade and Arn Harvey dropped in on the sheriff for a short visit and then repaired to the Widow Maker. Border Shift Brewster, red-faced and perspiring, with his mustache lamentably out of curl, greeted them with puffing enthusiasm.

"Never had such a day," he declared, "and they're still coming. This is going to be quite a night; let's have a drink on it."

Old Arn decided a snack was in order. While they were eating, a tall man dressed in black save for the snow of his ruffled shirt front came in and made his way to the bar.

Harvey eyed him speculatively.

"That's Steve Gore who bought the old Bradded L spread from Isaiah Dwyer, ain't it?" he remarked.

"That's right," Slade replied.

"The feller who works Mexicans and Yaquis?"

"Yes." Slade spoke quietly, but the manner in which he pronounced the single word caused old Arn to flush a little.

"I spent a night at his place," Slade continued. "He has a fine bunch of hands working for him and I found him pleasant and interesting. He's an up-and-coming cattleman, with progressive ideas that he's putting into practice. I've a notion the older spread owners of this section would do well to emulate him."

Harvey looked contemplative and tugged his mustache, a habit with him when he was thinking something out.

"He just spotted you and waved," he observed to Slade. "Suppose you ask him over to have a drink with us. I'd like to talk to him."

Slade relayed the invitation to Gore, who hesitated a moment and then accepted. He accompanied Slade to the table and sat down. Slade performed the introductions and the two cowmen shook hands. Each was a bit constrained at first, but they soon got to discussing the cattle business with progressive animation. Harvey was plainly impressed by the intelligence of Gore's answers to his questions and proceeded to ask more. Slade regarded the pair, a pleased expression in his gray eyes. He took little part in the conversation, being content to listen and watch the development of what he predicted would be a long and close friendship.

After a while Slade rose to his feet. "I'm going to take a little walk," he told his companions.

"Okay," nodded Harvey, "see you later. Take care of yourself, now."

Full dark had already fallen when Slade left the Widow Maker, but the air was fresh and cool, the sky glittering with stars. He strolled along the crowded street, enjoying the turbulent atmosphere. Every saloon was packed. There was a constant whirl and patter of conversation interspersed by the cheerful chink of bottle necks on glass rims and the sprightly ring of gold pieces on the mahogany. Strains of music drifted through the open windows as the perspiring musicians fiddled away for dear life. The clump of boots and the click of high heels sounded from the dance floors. Roulette wheels hummed and whirred, the little balls chittering in and out of the slots. Clouds of dust rose from the street as more and more riders stormed into town. Altogether, Sanders was doing itself proud in playing host to the throng of oil workers whose ambition seemed to be to get drunk and go broke as quickly as possible. Slade chuckled as he turned into a place now and then, hung around a few minutes and then continued his stroll.

At the far end of the main street was a saloon nearly as big as Border Shift Brewster's Widow Maker — the Hoot Owl. Why it was named that nobody ever took the trouble to find out.

The Hoot Owl differed from the Widow Maker, which was primarily a cattleman's hangout, in that it catered largely to the owners and workers of sheep ranches, of which there were a number to the southeast. Down there the pastures were hilly and rocky, very poor for cattle, but sheep thrived on them.

There was very little friction between cowmen and sheepmen in this part of the Nueces country, but just the same the two factions largely kept to themselves.

Sol Appleton who owned the Hoot Owl acted as a sort of banker for the herders, many of whom were Mexicans, keeping money entrusted to his care in a big iron safe in his back room. Sometimes, when a flock had been sold or a big wool shipment, there was a hefty passel of *dinero* in that old safe.

Slade had visited the Hoot Owl a few times and found it interesting. Finally in the course of his stroll he sighted the squat building which housed the saloon. Beyond, scattered over the prairie, were a number of 'dobes and shacks, some used for storage purposes, others empty, their tenants having moved to better quarters.

He was but a few paces from the saloon when he was almost knocked off his feet by the concussion of a thunderous explosion. On the prairie beyond the saloon blazed a yellowish flare. Deafened, half stunned, he sagged against a wall, his eyes dazzled by the glare.

Men were shouting and cursing as they streamed from bars and restaurants, and from the Hoot Owl in particular. Yelping questions and oaths, they pounded toward the scene of the explosion, where swiftly spreading flame flickered. Slade saw two white-aproned bartenders bring up the rear of the crowd pouring from the Hoot Owl. Shaking himself together, he was about to follow when he saw four men entering the saloon, walking swiftly and purposefully. Their hatbrims were drawn low over their eyes, their neckerchiefs muffled up about their chins.

Slade halted in mid stride staring at the still swinging doors. Why were those jiggers in such a hurry to get into a place everybody else was running out of? It looked sort of funny. He strode forward and slipped through the swinging doors and into the saloon, which was not very well lighted by two hanging lamps.

The bar and tables were deserted, the place emptied by the excitement of the explosion. Behind the bar stood Sol Appleton, his hands raised shoulder high. Beside him was a younger man, evidently one of his bartenders who had lingered behind when the others ran out; his hands were also in the air. Facing them were the four men who had just entered, drawn guns in their hands. They had jerked their black neckerchiefs up to cover their features, so that little more than the glint of eyes could be seen beneath the low drawn hatbrim.

"All right," one was in the act of saying, "open that safe in the back room and be quick about it."

Appleton, his usually florid face ashen,

started to move toward the far end of the bar. The four outlaws, intent on the business at hand, had failed to notice Slade's silent entrance. They jumped, whirling around, as his voice rang out.

"Drop those irons! You're covered!"

For an instant Slade thought they were going to obey the command. Then one whipped his gun in El Halcon's direction.

Slade grimly shot him. He reeled back with a yelp of pain, pawing at his blood-spurting shoulder. At the same instant one of his companions fired twice, not at Slade. The big hanging lamps flew to fragments. Black darkness blanketed the room, through which knifed an awful scream of agony and terror.

Weaving and ducking, Slade fired answering shots at the red spurts lancing the darkness. Bullets whined past him, thudding into the wall. He crouched low, shooting as fast as he could pull trigger. Then abruptly he realized no more lead was coming in his direction. Half deafened by the roar of his own guns, he dimly heard a patter of running feet, a sudden crashing sound, then silence. Thumbs hooked over the hammers of his guns, he bounded forward, tripped over a body sprawled on the floor and went down with a force that knocked the breath from his lungs. Gasping, he scrambled to his feet and stood listening but could hear nothing.

"Somebody get a light," he shouted as soon as he got enough wind.

There was a scratching and scuffling behind the bar, then a light flared. Sol Appleton was holding up a bracket lamp with a shaking hand.

"They went out the back door!" he bellowed.

Slade took the lamp from him and hurried around the end of the bar and through the door of the back room. It was empty save for a table, a couple of chairs and the big iron safe. An open door in the far wall showed where the outlaws had made their escape. Outside was only darkness dimly lighted by the fire set off by the explosion. There was nobody in sight. Slade went back to the saloon.

"Get some more lamps if you've got them," he told Appleton. "I want to have a good look at this jigger on the floor."

More lamps were quickly forthcoming. Slade jerked down the mask that covered the dead man's face, revealing a hard-looking face with already glazing eyes.

"Know him?" he asked Appleton.

"Never saw him before that I can remember," the saloonkeeper replied.

"Me neither," said the bartender.

Slade examined the mask. "Clever," he remarked. "An elastic band fitted at the back so it could be jerked up over the devil's face quickly and easily."

"The infernal Dawn Riders, sure as blazes!" declared Appleton.

"Maybe," Slade conceded, and continued his examination. Abruptly he realized that the right shoulder of the man's shirt was wet with blood, but that otherwise there appeared to be no bullet wound on him.

Slade stared at the corpse. "What the devil!" he exclaimed. "Whoever heard of a man cashing in from a slug through the top of his shoulder! Must have had a heart attack."

He probed about the fellow's breast for a possible wound he did not expect to find and didn't. He shook his head and turned the body over on its face, rocked back on his heels and stared again.

Driven to the hilt between the man's shoulder blades was a heavy knife.

Slade raised his eyes to Appleton and the bartender, who were hovering near, holding the lamps.

"Which one of you let him have it with that sticker?" he asked.

"Not me," Appleton instantly answered. "I hit the floor behind the bar when the shooting started."

"Me neither," said the bartender. "I was right down there alongside Sol."

Slade's lips pursed in a low whistle. "And it's sure for certain I didn't," he said.

"Then who the devil did?" demanded Appleton.

Slade straightened up, fished out his tobacco and papers and began rolling a cigarette.

"Well," he said, "besides we three the only gents in here were the three that came in with this one. It would appear one of them did it."

"But why would they knife one of their own bunch?" Appleton wondered.

"Hard to tell," Slade replied evasively. "Maybe one of them had a grudge against him, or it could have been an accident."

"One or the other, I reckon, but it sure don't seem to make sense," said the saloon-keeper, shaking his head in bewilderment.

"Well, anyhow, it did for him," Slade observed, lighting his cigarette.

"And a good thing!" growled Appleton. "I hope you winged the rest of them."

"Not likely," Slade said. "No blood spots on the floor and they moved mighty fast. If

I hadn't taken that header I might have caught up with them, but as it was they got in the clear."

Outside was a sound of voices. Men were returning from the scene of the explosion.

"Just an old shack out there on the prairie, blowed to bits by dynamite," one called. "Reckon some jigger thinks it's Fourth of July. It's burning itself out."

The men entering the saloon halted at the sight of the body on the floor, then began crowding around it, asking questions.

"Take it easy! Take it easy!" said Appleton. "I'll get some more lights in a minute. Charley, there are lamps in the stock room," he told the bartender.

"Here comes the sheriff," somebody shouted.

Sheriff Bascomb pushed his way through the crowd. He glanced inquiringly at Slade who had moved a little to one side.

"What the devil went on here?" he asked.

Appleton told him, volubly, to the accompaniment of exclamations from the crowd.

"Yes, they were going to make me open the safe," he concluded. "Slade got here just in time to stop 'em."

"Who let him have it with that sticker?"

173

asked the sheriff, his eyes on the knife handle.

"That's what we want to know," said Appleton. "Slade figures it must have been one of his own bunch. Reckon he's right. Neither him or me or Charley did, that's certain."

Sheriff Bascomb again glanced at Slade who shook his head slightly. The sheriff deftly changed the subject.

"What were they after, Sol?" he asked of the saloonkeeper.

"There's better than seven thousand dollars in my safe tonight," Appleton explained. "Alfredo Montez sold a flock today to a buyer here in town. He didn't want to be packing all that money around on him so he had me lock it up. Reckon somebody must have spotted him with it."

"Seems somebody always knows right where money happens to be in this section," growled the sheriff. "Okay, some of you fellers pack that carcass up to my office and lay it on the floor. There'll be a deputy in the office. I told him to stay there till I got back from finding out what that dang dynamite explosion was. You come along with me, Slade. I want to hear what you've got to say about it."

They left the saloon together, several men

following with the body. When they were out of earshot, Bascomb turned to Slade.

"Got another one, eh?" he remarked.

"Another one was got," Slade corrected. "I just put a slug through his shoulder."

"And you figure one of the bunch did it?"

"That's exactly what happened," Slade replied.

"But why?" demanded the sheriff.

"That fellow was hard hit," Slade explained. "He couldn't have gotten away with the rest, so one of them made sure he wouldn't be captured and possibly talk.

"If that's the answer, and I'm pretty certain it is," he added, "it was sure fast thinking on the part of somebody, faster even than shooting out the lights first off."

"A smooth sidewinder, all right," growled the sheriff.

"Well, anyhow they didn't get by with what they planned this time," Slade said, "and knifing that hellion convinces me of what I've been suspecting for some time, that a local man of considerable prominence is at the head of the outfit."

"Any notion who?" asked the sheriff.

"Yes, I have a notion," Slade replied slowly, "but it's only a notion, so far, with nothing on which to base it, and if I'm right it's one of the most fantastic schemes I ever heard tell of. Simple, yes, but utterly ingenious. I'm also getting a vague notion as to how to drop a loop on the sidewinder."

Sheriff Bascomb looked expectant, but Slade did not carry the discussion further.

"How'd you get hep to what was going on?" Bascomb asked.

"It looked strange to me that those four jiggers should be in such a hurry to get into the place everybody else was in a devil of a hurry to get out of," Slade answered. "And they had a look about them that I figured didn't bode any good for somebody. So I just slid in after them, and there they were, holding guns on Appleton and his bartender and ordering him to open the safe."

The sheriff nodded. "And you think you may have an idea how to corral the big hewolf of the pack?" he hinted.

Slade smiled slightly. "Yes, I have," he admitted, "but I'm bothered about one thing. I've a notion the hellion may be figuring on pulling out. If he does and gets south of the Border, for instance, he's gone. And right now there isn't a thing I can do to stop him, not even if I watched him ride away."

Sheriff Bascomb swore and shook his head. "Well, here's hoping something will break for us," he said.

"I'm afraid we'll have to make the breaks,"

Slade answered. "About the nearest to one we've had so far was me happening to be down in that end of town when they set off the dynamite explosion to clear everybody out of the saloon. Can't very well hope for another such fortunate coincidence. Well, we'll see."

The body of the dead outlaw was placed on view. The news of the attempted robbery had already spread around and people began trooping into the office. Slade was not at all surprised when nobody was able to identify the dead man. There were the usual vague remembrances on the part of bartenders and others, which Slade was inclined to discount as figments of lively imaginations. It was only Steve Gore who was able to produce anything definite.

"I'm pretty sure I met this fellow riding the lower trail one day," he remarked. "He turned off at that branch which leads to the northeast, six or seven miles south of town."

This bit of information Slade stowed away in a corner of his mind for future consideration.

Sixteen

When Slade rode away from the Diamond H ranchhouse the following day he forked a rangy sorrel of speed and endurance, and the sorrel's rig was equipped with a saddle boot. He would have preferred Shadow for the chore he had in mind, but to take out the big black ostensibly to comb thorny pastures would have attracted notice and perhaps occasioned comment; a cowboy does not risk his pet saddle horse's legs on such work.

Slade rode west by slightly north and eventually he topped a tall, brush covered ridge from the crest of which he could look down into a wide, valley-like depression where sat an old ranchhouse in a grove of pinons. It was, he knew, Miles Pacer's Booger F *casa*. He dismounted, hobbled the sorrel in a little cleared place where there was grass and made himself comfortable. He passed the afternoon watching the activities in the hollow below. He saw Booger F cowhands ride away from the ranch, others ride in, and saw Miles Pacer pottering about the various buildings. Not until the shadows were long did he quit his post and ride back to the Diamond H, with nothing accomplished.

"Just the same I've got a hunch that digging down there will bear a bit of watching," he told the sorrel who, not understanding man-talk as well as Shadow, looked a bit puzzled.

It was different the next day, however. Shortly after noon the entire Booger F outfit rode off toward the north pastures. Only Miles Pacer was left sitting on the front veranda. An hour later Slade spotted a single horseman riding up from the southwest, following a trail that wound into the shallow valley. In front of the Booger F ranchhouse he dismounted, leaving his horse standing. He and Pacer entered the ranchhouse. Some little time passed before they reappeared. Pacer remained on the porch; the horseman rode off the way he had come.

From his elevation, Slade watched him grow small in the distance, still riding the trail. With a final glance at the silent ranchhouse, he secured his horse and rode swiftly down the slope until he reached the trail. The man had vanished from sight, but the trail ran on through the thorny pastures and Slade felt that it was unlikely that he would turn aside. He continued at a good pace up a long slope. As he neared the crest he slowed down a bit, keeping in the shadow as much as possible.

From the crest of the rise he sighted his quarry riding across the level ground at the foot of the sag and toward a canyon mouth the trail entered. Slade waited until he had disappeared within the gloomy gorge and again took up the pursuit. It was a bit ticklish, riding across the open lowland, for if the fellow really had something off-color in mind he would quite likely look with suspicion on anybody riding his track and might display his disapproval with a slug. But nothing happened and he entered the canyon mouth and rode on, every sense alert and vigilant. He knew he was now among the bleak gorges and gulches that slashed the grim environs of lonely San Cajo, the hangout for owlhoots for many years, where the caves said to be their hideouts bored into the water fissured limestone of the cliffs.

The trail wound on through the canyon that emptied into a second cutting its course at right-angles, and again he saw the solitary horseman riding up still another slope that was broken by a series of benches forming small mesas. Slade waited until the heavy chaparral growth swallowed him and sent the sorrel drifting across the gorge. He had gained on his quarry and he rode more slowly and with greater caution. Well up the sag, which was more than two miles in extent, the trail abruptly veered due south along the slope, which was really the beginning of San Cajo's thorny breast.

The trail was very faint and old, but the keen eyes of El Halcon noted signs that it had been ridden quite a few times of late.

For a mile or more the track wound through the thick brush, then gradually the growth began to thin; Slade redoubled his caution. From time to time he pulled the sorrel to a halt and sat listening. At last, when the brush was becoming disquietingly scattered, in one of his moments of pause he heard, no great distance ahead, the click of a horse's irons on hard soil. Abruptly the sound ceased. Slade eased his horse into the brush, halting him where the growth was thin. He dismounted, stood listening for a moment and then stole forward through the chaparral, paralleling the trail.

Scantier and scantier grew the straggle of leaves and branches. Slade halted at a final fringe, pressed the twigs gently aside and before him lay a clearing of some yards in extent. A slope tumbled down from its outer lip. The other side of the open space was walled by a beetling cliff and at the base of the cliff was an opening into which was fitted a ponderous wooden door now standing half open. Before the door stood a horse; its rider was nowhere in sight. Presumably he was in the cave or chamber hollowed out in the rock.

For a good twenty minutes Slade stood gazing at the silent opening. Abruptly the man he had been trailing appeared, carrying what looked to be a canvas sack which he balanced across the front of his saddle. He turned back to the opening, swung the door shut and dropped a heavy iron bar into brackets set into the stone. Then he mounted the horse and headed back the way by which he had entered the clearing. Crouched in his hiding place, Slade saw him pass. He was a heavy-set man with a bristling black beard that hid most of his face; his hat was pulled low over his eyes.

Slade stood motionless until the faint thud of hoofs on the trail died away. Then he debated swiftly what to do. Should he follow the quarry or should he try and find out what was on the other side of that wooden door? Evidently there was nobody inside or the fellow would hardly have dropped the bar in place. Also it was fairly logical to believe he was headed back to the Booger F ranchhouse with whatever it was he had come to fetch. And Slade's curiosity as to what appeared to be a hidden hangout was at white heat.

Curiosity won. He stood listening for a few minutes longer and, reassured by the continued silence, slipped across the clearing to the door. Unbarring it, he swung it open and peered into a shadowy chamber perhaps twenty feet square and, whether of natural origin or hewn in the rock he was unable to determine. At first he could see but little, then as his eyes accustomed themselves to the gloom he stepped through the opening and glanced about.

The room was empty of furnishings but there was evidence of recent occupancy. Along one wall were several husk bed ticks and tumbled blankets. A few cooking utensils were in evidence and some tin plates and cups. There were the ashes of a fire. A couple of lanterns stood nearby.

In the far wall was a second door, standing ajar. Slade walked across and pulled it open to reveal a second and smaller chamber. He could dimly make out still a third wooden door in the opposite wall, this one closed, but apparently neither barred nor bolted. Very little light reached the inner chamber. He turned back, picked up one of the lanterns and shook it. The bowl appeared full of oil. He touched a match to the wick and returned to the inner room. The yellowish glow showed a heap of strange odds and ends. There were what appeared to be altar candlesticks, stained and discolored. From their weight he judged them to be of gold. Scattered about were the rotting rags of ancient finery, also the remains of leather bridles and saddles of an antique fashion and studded with turquoise, the irons either of silver or heavily plated with that metal. Without doubt the cave had once been the hangout of one of the robber gangs of bygone days that preyed on traffic from Laredo to San Antonio by way of the old lower trail. And it had evidently been recently used as a hideout by some other similar bunch, quite likely the notorious Dawn Riders.

Slade straightened up from his inspection of the remnants of ancient loot. He was turning toward the outer chamber when a thunderous crash quivered the air, followed by a clang of metal on metal and a burst of raucous, derisive laughter. Slade bounded through the doorway. The light filtering into the big cave had been snuffed out. Instead of an opening to the outer air, the timbers of the massive front door met his gaze. He hurled his weight against the barrier but he might as well have butted against the rock walls of the cave for all the results he got. Again came the discordant laughter, farther away this time, then silence.

Slade placed the lantern on the floor,

leaned against the wall and fished out the makin's. He was in a very bad temper as he rolled and lighted a cigarette, his anger directed chiefly at himself. Too late he realized that in his eagerness to explore the hideout, he had blithely walked into a cleverly baited trap. Doubtless the man he trailed knew all the time that somebody was on his track, knew perhaps just who that somebody was. Perhaps he, Slade, had been spotted keeping watch on the Booger F ranchhouse and the man had ridden off for the express purpose of luring him to the cave. Smart enough, too, to come out with a sack full of something, presumably the reason for his visit to the hideout. With belated understanding, Slade saw how the fellow reasoned that curiosity would induce him to enter the cave. He had slipped back, made sure he, Slade, was occupied inside and had slammed and barred the door.

Had he gone to fetch companions? Slade reasoned it was highly unlikely. The armed prisoner, with the inner room for sanctuary, would be too able to give an excellent account of himself against a frontal attack. No, he had no intention of returning with or without others. Slade had a grim premonition that nothing so swift and merciful as a bullet was in mind for him.

He examined the door and decided quickly that it was far beyond his ability to break down even with a battering ram if he had one, which he didn't. It was constructed of roughly squared logs of considerable size. Burn his way through? No chance. It would take a large amount of kindling to heat the dampish logs enough to start them blazing. And kindling, or anything that would serve for it, was conspicuous by its absence. And a careful search of the cave showed there was not a scrap of food or a drop of water.

Slade did not get exactly panicky, but the cold chill that formed around his heart was not pleasant. To all appearances he was due for death by thirst and slow starvation. Nobody at the Diamond H had the slightest notion where he had gone, even before he followed the horseman into San Cajo's wild fastness of gorges and canyons. The sorrel horse would before long find his way back to the ranchhouse and his feed bag, but nobody would know where he came from. There would doubtless be a search for his body, which wouldn't be found.

Suddenly he remembered the third door, the one in the far wall of the inner room. He picked up the lantern, crossed to it and swung it wide. It opened onto a dark and rather narrow tunnel which Slade eyed with little hope. Highly unlikely that it led to anything promising. If it did, there would have been nothing to gain by imprisoning him in the cave.

Nevertheless, he decided to explore the forbidding-looking bore. Better than doing nothing and there was always the faint chance that it might provide a route of escape, perhaps a concealed one overlooked by the outlaws who had very likely also explored it. Making sure the lantern bowl was full of oil he set out.

The corridor was irregular and contorted in shape and course, which gave it the appearance of having been blown bodily in the mountain by some frightful eruption of gas following the line of least resistance. Or perhaps it had been hollowed out by the gnawing force of water through untold ages. Now, however, it was perfectly dry. The air was thick and heavy but breatheable.

As Slade progressed, he noted that the slope of the passage, while slight, was persistently downward, which was not encouraging, suggesting as it did that the burrow plunged into the bowels of the earth without any second opening to the outer air.

After what seemed a very long time the corridor levelled off. It turned and twisted, changing its course so frequently that soon he was utterly confused as to direction and began to experience an eerie feeling that he was continually travelling in a circle and getting nowhere at all.

Another hour of weary trudging along the echoing gallery and he gradually became conscious of a low, persistent sound. At first he thought it was but the blood roaring in his veins, audible because of the surrounding utter silence, or a ringing of the ears set up by the heavy atmosphere. But the sound increased in volume, grew from a murmur to a deep droning, swelled to a weird plaint interspersed by uncanny shrieks and wails. Slade was at a loss to account for the origin of the unexplainable tumult.

Suddenly it seemed to him that the black darkness ahead was graying slightly. He was inclined to attribute it to overwrought imagination, but the faint light undoubtedly increased as he forged ahead. Soon he could vaguely make out the walls of the corridor. The ghostly sounds also increased until the rock walls seemed to quiver under their impact. A moment later and he saw that the tunnel had come to an end.

But what an end! Slade's scalp prickled as he stared at the weird scene before him.

The tunnel opened into a mighty chasm

in the black rock, jagged and torn and splintered, as if in some dim, distant age of the past a terrific lightning bolt had cloven the cliffs like a flaming sword of vengeance, leaving this ghastly wound behind. The opposite cliff of the chasm was swatched in blackness and the exact width of the gulf it was impossible to determine.

Slade glanced up. Far, far above, fully two thousand feet, he estimated, was a narrow ribbon of blue sky, from which heavy dregs of light seeped to the depths in which he stood. The gloom of the chasm was the gloom of a closely-shuttered room in the daytime.

How far down it extended from the lip of the corridor he could not tell, but the impenetrability of the darkness hinted at tremendous depths.

And rising from the lip of the corridor, and of a width almost as great, was a stupendous natural bridge of dark stone.

Up and outward soared the mighty arc in a titanic curve. Beyond the apex of the arc the far cliff overhung, shutting out even the feeble light that struggled down from the heights, and the bridge beyond the point was invisible, giving the impression of a prodigious half-arc suspended in the arms of the darkness.

Down the gulf great winds dashed and roared, driving misty wreaths and clouds of vapor before them, until the cyclopean span hummed and moaned like a giant harp. Wailings and shriekings arose as the gusts tore through crevices in the splintered stone, and the echoing cliffs magnified the sound a thousandfold, until it seemed that a concourse of demons from the Pit was holding high revel in the darksome cleft.

For long minutes Slade stood staring at the awful scene. Then he shrugged his shoulders and stepped boldly onto the causeway of the bridge.

Instantly he was exposed to the full force of the tearing wind. He reeled, staggered, kept his balance with difficulty. Then, bending almost double, he crept cautiously up the gentle slope of the arc, holding the flickering lantern well in front of him, examining each foot of stone before he trusted his weight upon it. It was fortunate that he had a lantern with a globe rather than a torch, which the wind would have instantly extinguished.

He had covered much more than a hundred paces before he reached the apex of the arc. Here the gloom lessened somewhat and he quickened his pace. Fifty yards farther on, just before he reached the downward curve of the span, he halted abruptly.

Now he understood why the outlaw who locked him in the cave had no fear of his escaping by way of the tunnel which opened into it. At his feet was a crevice fifteen or sixteen feet in width and downward into the mass of the rock for an unknown distance. Slade crept to the splintered side edge of the bridge and gazed downward into depth upon vertiginous depth that seemed to extend to the heart of earth itself. In the gulf moved vast mist shadows, writhing and coiling as if in torment.

Shaken, giddy, he moved back from the edge and stood on the lip of the crevice in the bridge floor, measuring its width with his eye, carefully examining to the best of his ability in the uncertain light the condition of the ground on the far side of the cleft. It appeared sound enough although broken and uneven. Shaking his head, he crept to the other side edge of the bridge. And again before him was that pitiless gulf of darkness and eerie shadows. There was only one possible way to get across the crevice — jump it!

Such an attempt seemed utterly absurd, nothing less than a particularly awful way to commit suicide. In fact it would have been just that for a man of average height and strength, a conclusion doubtless arrived at by the outlaw who imprisoned him. But Slade's great length of limb and far more than average strength and activity decreased to a degree the apparently impossible odds. There was a chance, a faint one, he had to admit, but a chance that he might be able to clear the gulf. Rolling a cigarette with difficulty and finally managing to light it, he considered the matter with a concentration that amounted to mental agony.

The distance, he decided, was indeed not more than fifteen feet. In his college days he had jumped twenty and better, but certainly not under such awesome conditions. A splintered, jagged lip of rock, in a half darkness of shifting shadows and with a hurricane of gusty wind tearing and thrusting at him, to take off from; a gulf of unknown depth to clear, and a landing place of broken, uneven stone! He drew a deep breath and hesitated.

After all, however, there wasn't much choice before him. It was a case of risking a quick death in the air against a certain slow one by starvation in the tunnel. And if he managed to clear the crevice and reach the continuation of the tunnel on the far side of the bridge, there was always the possibility that it might finally emerge somewhere. He had already been encouraged by the fact that for some time the bore had developed an upward trend. Yes, he might as well take the chance; he had nothing to lose and everything to gain.

Regretfully he set the lantern aside, consoling himself with the thought that anyhow the oil must be very nearly exhausted. Then he retraced his steps for a score of yards, breathed deeply and ran forward at full speed.

The mighty wind whipped and tore at him. The wild storm voices, set to the deep undertone of the humming span, howled a warning and a threat. The shadows crawled and shifted. The crumbling rock turned beneath his feet.

He reached the lip of the crevice and sprang wildly out into the dizzy air; he did not expect to live five seconds longer. A horrible sense of despair shot through his brain as he realized he had jumped short.

SEVENTEEN

For what seemed untold ages, Slade shot through the screaming air and plunged downward, his clutching hands outstretched. As he hurtled into the depths his arms and his hands slammed against the opposite lip of the cleft with numbing force. The fingers of one hand closed about a knob of rock and stopped his downward progress with a jerk that almost tore his arm from the socket.

For an instant that was an eternity of terror and pain-streaked effort he swung to and fro, with the clawing shadows all around him and the hideous depths beneath. Then he managed to stretch his other arm out far enough to grasp a second knob of stone. He hung for an instant gasping, and gathering strength for a supreme attempt. Slowly, gradually, every powerful muscle quivering with strain, he drew himself up till his breast was resting on the rough stone of the bridge floor. Another writhe and struggle and he lay at full length upon the vibrating causeway, his nerves tautened to agonizing tenseness, perspiration streaming from every pore, his breath coming in choking gulps.

For a long time he lay motionless, until his strength returned and his tortured nerves got back to something like normal. Then he rose to his feet, rather shakily, and looked about him.

The first thing he noted was that the floor of the bridge dipped sharply downward almost from the lip of the crevice. There was no going back the way he came; it would be impossible to get up enough speed on the steeply slanting surface to clear the gap. Nowhere to go but ahead, and he devoutly prayed that the infernal coyote hole didn't end in a blank wall.

He glanced back at the dim and flickering glow of the abandoned lantern, waved it a derisive farewell and began groping his way down the descent, leaning against the gusts of wind, cautiously testing the ground ahead at each step.

As he had surmised, the far end of the bridge ended in a continuation of the tunnel. When he reached it he could just make out the darker opening yawning amid the shadows. Another moment and the giant wind and the wailing voices of the gulf were behind him, which was a relief because the never-ceasing uproar was hard on the nerves.

For a while he proceeded cautiously, testing the ground ahead, but finally he grew too weary to care and plodded doggedly onward, heedless of possible pitfalls, only taking the precaution continuously to brush one hand against the rock wall to anticipate the passage's devious windings. Once he heard the sound of rushing water nearby, but though he was parched with thirst, he dared not attempt to reach it, for it evidently flowed some distance below the path he was following. He hugged the rock wall closely until the sound died out behind him. Hour after hour he plodded on. He was blind with fatigue when once again the premonitory grayness shaded the darkness ahead. He quickened his step, rounded a turn and stood dazzled by a bar of intense light that streamed across the corridor.

The light poured through an opening in the cave wall that rent the rock at about shoulder height. It was hardly larger than a window.

Slade managed to scramble up to it, wormed his way through and found himself standing on a shelf of stone with a sheer cliff falling away at his feet to the floor of a canyon some sixty feet below. The far wall of the canyon, a half mile distant, was ablaze with golden morning sunlight; he had been wandering all night in those torturous worm-holes of stone.

About a dozen feet below the edge of the opening, the cliff bulged outward, but beyond the rounded edge of the bulge he could see a gleam of water below.

The water looked cool and inviting and he was conscious that his greatest desire was for a drink.

He examined the cliff face on either side of the opening. It was perfectly sheer. A lizard would have experienced difficulty negotiating a descent. He turned his gaze back to the water; it looked deep but might be dangerously shallow. That rocky bank of the stream was but a few yards distant.

The height was not excessive for a dive, but the bulge of the cliff presented a disquieting hazard. Should his body strike the bulge in the course of its descent, he would doubtless be hurled far enough out from the cliff to miss the water and be dashed to death on the stones of the bank.

But once again he had scant alternative. The only one was to re-enter that dreary cave and continue his painful plodding along its winding burrow, with no guarantee that another opening, easier to negotiate would be present. It was that, or risk the dive.

Slade didn't take long to make up his mind. He decided he had had enough of that infernal badger hole through the rock, and if he was going to cash in, he preferred to do so under the sun rather than in the clammy darkness of the cave. He leaned against the stone and rested for a brief period, then he gathered himself together and leaped far out from the shelf's edge and shot downward through the screaming air.

He cleared the bulge with scant inches to spare and an instant later vanished into the water with a sullen plunge.

Down, down he sank, until he thought he would never rise again, until his chest was bursting for want of air and waves of blackness were crowding down upon him. Then slowly he began to rise. He broke surface with a gasp of relief, gulped great draughts of life-giving air and began struggling towards the bank, which was but a short distance away.

But the water was icy cold and the current ran like a millrace with a tendency to sweep him back toward where the stream washed the perpendicular wall of the cliff with no beach between it and the water's edge. Hampered by his clothes and his heavy guns, and weak with weariness, he swam sluggishly and for several hundred yards he hardly gained a foot. Then, with his strength rapidly failing and a feeling of numb disregard for consequences creeping over him, he at last felt his boot soles crunch on the gravelly bottom. A moment later he crawled onto the shingly beach and lay utterly exhausted.

The sun had risen higher and its warmth quickly beat the chill from his bones and steamed his drenched clothes. His strength revived and he managed to drag off his boots and outer garments and free them of most of the water. Donning the still damp clothes, which would dry more comfortably on his body, and making sure his guns were in working condition, he rested a few minutes longer and then painfully climbed the steep bank to the canyon floor.

He had not the least notion where he was and decided to follow the stream down-canyon. He was sore all over, aching in every bone and deathly tired, but nevertheless he was in an exultant frame of mind. The happenings of the past twenty-four hours had substantiated unequivocally his estimate of the man he had come to suspect, Miles Pacer. No longer was there the slightest doubt in his mind but that there was something decidedly off-color about Miles Pacer. The man who had attempted to murder him by slow starvation in the cave had just come from a consultation with Pacer. Of course there was still no proof that Pacer had anything to do with the attempt. In fact, there was no proof against Pacer where anything was conconcerned. But Slade was now convinced in his own mind and he felt that he would be able, before long, to prove Pacer guilty of perpetrating a fraud. He was also pretty well convinced that Pacer and no other was the brains of the mysterious outlaw band known as the Dawn Riders, although he was forced to admit that would still take some proving. However, he felt that it was now in his power to very likely cause Pacer to tip his hand.

He reviewed certain incidents relative to Pacer, of little apparent moment at the time, but attaining significance in the light of future developments. Pacer's sudden and unexpected departure from the Diamond H ranchhouse the evening before he, Slade, was ambushed on the trail to Sanders. His equally unexpected failure to return to the Widow Maker the day of the oil field robbery and his reappearance the following morning showing signs of a hard and sleepless night which he glibly explained, without invitation to do so, as the results of a session of drinking and poker. Little things at the time, but now looming large. More pleased than otherwise, Slade strode on, seeking a point where he would be able to get his bearings.

After several miles of trudging he reached a spot where the perpendicular walls on the near side of the gorge were replaced by a long slope that slanted steeply upward. He slowly climbed the rocky sag to its crest.

From this vantage he could see many miles in every direction, a vista of jumbled hills and canyons thickly grown with prickly pear and *granjeno.* To the northeast, perhaps a score of miles distant, was what looked like a film of dark cloud lying along the blue slant of the sky. It was undoubtedly the smoke smudge that marked the site of Sanders. Slade decided that if he bore to the right he should within a few miles strike the lower trail that ran past the Diamond H ranchhouse.

He set out, scrambling down the opposite slope, and after a long and weary tramp saw the gray ribbon of the trail lying along the base of the ridge he was descending. Reaching it he headed north, limping painfully in his high-heeled boots.

Before he had gone a mile he heard a sound behind him. Glancing back he saw a line of freighting wagons rumbling up from the south. He stopped and waited for them to approach. As they drew near, the driver of the foremost wagon picked up a rifle leaning against the seat beside him. His gaze was distinctly dubious, but as Slade stood quietly beside the trail, his hands hanging by his sides, he put the long gun down and let out a shout.

"What the devil you doing out here on shanks' mare, cowboy?" he asked. "I thought cowhands never walked."

"Got off my horse back in the hills, and that was the last I saw of him," Slade replied, with perfect truth. "How's chances for a lift to the Diamond H, this side of town?"

The driver looked him up and down, still a bit suspicious, but evidently decided he appeared okay.

"All right," he said, "hop up here with me. Everybody's jumpy along this devilish trail," he explained apologetically as Slade gratefully climbed to the seat. "Those infernal Dawn Riders and their sort are liable to pop up anywhere. Not that they'd get anything from this train but hides and wool and tallow. You look like you've been in the water."

"Had to swim a creek to reach the trail," Slade replied, again with truth.

The driver, evidently a taciturn individual, nodded and turned his attention to his horses. Slade dozed comfortably on the wide seat till the driver nudged him as the shadows were growing long.

"Your stop's right around the next bend," he said.

A little later Slade thanked the driver for his kindness and dropped to the ground in front of the Diamond H ranchhouse. As he walked slowly up the drive, Audrey appeared on the veranda.

"Heavenly days! Not again!" she exclaimed.

"Yep, once again," Slade replied. "Did my horse get here ahead of me this time?"

"No, thank goodness. At least I was spared that. What in the world happened?"

Slade told her briefly, leaving out most of the harrowing details and refraining from mentioning Miles Pacer or where he started trailing the suspect.

Audrey shook her head and sighed resignedly. "Come on out to the kitchen and I'll fix you something to eat," she said. "You must be starved. Dad should be back by dark."

Slade had hardly finished eating the food she prepared, to which he did full justice for he was famished, when old Arn rode in. He repeated the story for the ranchowner's benefit. Harvey commented profanely.

"And now, sir, I want you to do something," Slade said.

"Anything you ask," Harvey acceded at once.

"I want you to ride to town and get Sancho Rojas and bring him here," Slade explained. "And while you're at it, drop in at the county surveyor's office and borrow a surveyor's compass, a Jacob's staff to serve in lieu of a tripod to support the compass, and a surveyor's tape or an engineer's chain. You can do that?"

"Sure for certain," Harvey promised. "I'll take care of everything."

He gazed at Slade. "Figure to make a try for that sand flat where my brothers were killed?" he asked.

"Guess that's the idea," Slade admitted.

"And do you believe there's something really worth looking for?"

"I've a notion we'll find something that will surprise you," Slade replied evasively.

"But nobody knows where to look for that infernal flat," Harvey protested.

"There is somebody who knows how to find it," Slade answered.

"Who?"

"Remember the Mexican boy who went along with your brothers?" Slade asked.

Harvey nodded. "Uh-huh, I remember him. A scrawny little squirt."

"Well," Slade answered. "Sancho Rojas was that boy."

Old Arn stared. "Well, I'll be darned!" he exclaimed. "But why didn't he ever tell anybody? He's been living in this section for years and nobody ever heard him mention a word about it."

"Rojas, just a boy then, was terribly frightened by what happened," Slade explained. "He was superstitious and figured ghosts or evil spirits had a hand in it. He ran away and didn't come back to the section until years had passed and he'd been educated in a mission and had gotten over most of his fear of supernatural beings. Then I guess he didn't see any sense of stirring up old memories he figured were best forgotten. He did tell a friend of his a year or so back, and that friend went right out and got himself killed. I think that gave Rojas considerable of a scare, and perhaps revived something of his former fear of evil spirits. But he'll guide us to the flat if I ask him to."

"This darn business gets mixed up more and more all the time," complained Harvey, "but I'll string along with you. I've always been a bit curious about that old map myself. Maybe we'll find out once and for all if there really was anything to the yarn. Okay, I'll take care of everything. Now you'd better get to bed. You look dead on your feet."

"I am, darn near," Slade admitted. He mounted the stairs without further argument and ten minutes later was sleeping the sodden sleep of utter exhaustion.

When he awoke, Slade found himself still stiff and sore but otherwise little the worse for his frightful experience. But as he dressed, he suffered an uneasy feeling that the night before, his mind fogged by fatigue, he might have erred in not cautioning Arn Harvey to wait till darkness fell before slipping Sancho Rojas out of Sanders. He consoled himself with the thought that it was unlikely his departure would be observed by anyone with an interest in him.

EIGHTEEN

Harvey and Sancho arrived shortly after Slade had finished his breakfast.

"Yes, I will have no difficulty locating the sand flat," Sancho assured him. "I cannot perhaps find the exact spot where we dug."

"I'll take care of that," Slade replied, examining the compass and the Jacob's staff Harvey had procured. "All you need to do is guide us to the flat. How far would you say it is?"

"A long day's ride to the southeast," Sancho answered.

"We'll start in the morning," Slade decided.

They did start in the morning, leading a

pack horse loaded with tools and provisions, finally following the vestiges of a very old trail that wound southward through canyons and gorges and dense growths of chaparral. And as they rode there drifted along well behind them a single horseman who took the greatest care to remain undetected but who never lost sight of them. It was the bearded man who locked Slade in the cave. From time to time he would shake his head and mutter oaths. It was plain that he was much puzzled over how his captive had managed to escape; but in his eyes was the malicious satisfaction of one who foresees evil plans soon to bear fruit.

The sun was setting in scarlet and gold and the waters of the bay were flaming purple when Slade, Harvey and Sancho reached the edge of a desolate sand flat hemmed in by thickets. Over to one side, at the very brink of the water, towered a dark spire of stone upon which the dying sunlight glinted redly. The three pulled their horses to a halt and sat for a moment gazing across the quiet scene. And on the crest of a rise well to their rear, the shadow that had followed them all the long day turned his horse and rode swiftly back the way he had come.

"This is it without a doubt, *Señores,*" said

Sancho. "The passing years have wrought but little change."

"But the map says there are two chimney rocks and I don't see but one," protested old Arn. "Fact is I'm pretty sure here's the place the surveyor and me looked over when we rode this way."

"I think I'll be able to explain the missing rock," Slade said. He spoke to Shadow and they rode forward until they were beside the tall spire of stone. It was not really a chimney rock, although it looked like one, being, in fact, but a fang of harder strata that had resisted the erosion which in the course of ages wore down the parent reef to its present height.

Slade sighted along the water's edge. At a distance that he estimated at a thousand paces or so, was a jumble of rocks, some in and some out of the water. He led the way to the scattering of fragments over which the waters of the bay washed in frothy white. With a slight laugh he pointed to a jagged stub that rose a few feet above the level of the main ledge.

"Sancho, I believe you said there was a bad storm that night, didn't you?" he remarked.

"That is so," agreed the Mexican.

"With wind and lots of thunder and lightning?"

"Yes, it was a most terrible storm," Sancho answered. "The lightning was frightful and I never heard such thunder."

Slade gestured to the stub of stone and the scattering of broken fragments.

"That's what's left of your chimney rock," he said. "A bolt of lightning struck it and shattered it."

"By gosh, I believe you're right!" exclaimed Harvey.

"No doubt about it," Slade said. "Well, it's too late to get anything much done tonight. We'll make camp in one of those thickets and get an early start in the morning."

They utilized the remaining light to make camp and then slept soundly beside a smoldering fire until daybreak. The sun was just peeping over the eastern horizon when they got to work.

With Sancho standing on the stub of stone to give him a better mark, Slade took his sights, ran his measurements and made his calculations with great care, checking and re-checking the results and taking into consideration the probable height of the missing chimney rock; for he reasoned that the old map, presumably drawn by a sea captain familiar with instruments of navigation, would be quite accurate. He plotted the bisecting lines and designated the spot to dig.

"How big was that hole you fellows dug?" he asked Sancho.

"Just big enough for two men to work," Rojas replied.

"We'll make ours ten feet long and five wide," Slade said. "That should take care of any slight error and while it'll mean a bit more work I figure we'll have better luck that way."

They set to work with the picks and spades they had brought in the *aparejo* of the pack horse. All day long they toiled under the sun, deepening the broad and long hole until they were forced to use a rough ladder which they constructed on the spot to get in and out. Evening was drawing near when Sancho suddenly straightened his aching back and sniffed sharply.

"Capitan," he exclaimed, "the smell!"

Slade reached over and plucked Sancho's lighted cigarette from his lips and snuffed it out.

"No more smoking from now on," he cautioned. "Otherwise we may find ourselves out in the middle of the bay."

"What is it?" asked Harvey.

"Natural gas," Slade replied. "I was pretty sure of it after listening to Sancho describe his symptoms when he breathed it in the course of the former digging. That's why I planned this hole long and wide, to give the fumes a better chance to dissipate. It's a wonder Sancho and Pacer didn't die in that badger burrow they dug, and the Harveys, too, if they'd tried to get them out after they collapsed. Undoubtedly there is a great reservoir of natural gas under pressure beneath the flat, and very likely a big oil pool also. We'll discuss it later. Keep on digging."

A few minutes later Sancho swore feebly as his spade turned up something white.

"Bones!" he gasped.

Slade nodded without surprise; his eyes were glowing. "Keep on digging," he directed.

A moment more and his spade rang on metal.

"Ha! the treasure chest!" ejaculated Sancho. *"Sangre de Cristi!"* he added, his eyes bulging.

It wasn't a treasure chest, it was a rusty sixgun gripped in the bones of a skeleton hand. Old Arn peered close.

"Say," he exclaimed, "that ain't the sort of iron those pirate fellers packed. That's a

Colt Forty-four."

"Yes," Slade said quietly, "the gun that killed your two brothers. Keep on digging."

Muttering under his mustache, Harvey plied his spade. Sancho's face was beaded with sweat and he looked more than a little scared.

At the third stroke of Harvey's spade there was a gleam of gold. He leaned forward eagerly and scraped away with vigor.

A second bony hand came to light. On one fleshless finger was a broad gold band.

"Hold everything!" Slade said. He gently removed the ring, polished it on his overalls, inside and out, and held it to the light. Then he silently passed it to Harvey.

There was an inscription cut in the inner surface of the band and still plainly legible. Harvey read, "To Dirk from Alice."

Harvey raised his bewildered face and stared at Slade. "But — but what does it mean?" he asked.

"It means," Slade replied quietly, "that what we've uncovered is the skeleton of Dirk Pacer."

"But — but Dirk Pacer died in Mexico," protested Harvey. "His son, Miles Pacer, said so."

"The man who calls himself Miles Pacer is not Dirk Pacer's son, and he never lived in Mexico," Slade replied.

Harvey's jaw sagged and he looked utterly dumfounded. Sancho swore weakly in Spanish. Slade leaned against the wall of the pit to rest his back and wished for the cigarette he didn't dare light.

"Dirk Pacer was killed in the fight with your brothers," he explained. "He either fell back into the hole or the rising tide washed his body in and covered it with sand. My deduction is that in some manner Miles Pacer, as we will call him, heard the story of the treasure hunt and the fight. Perhaps from Sancho's friend to whom Sancho told the story. Perhaps the friend told it to somebody else who talked to the wrong pair of ears. Perhaps he was overheard telling it by somebody associated with Miles Pacer. Anyhow, Miles Pacer formed the same conclusion that I eventually arrived at — that Dirk Pacer was killed in the course of the fight and that his bones were here on the sand flat. Remember, the Dawn Riders were operating in this section before Miles Pacer put in an appearance. My conclusion is that Miles Pacer, the brains of the Dawn Riders, figured out a neat little scheme to get hold of a valuable property and at the same time have a safe and convenient base from which to conduct operations. As a prosperous and well-thought of ranchowner, he was in a position to get information and learn where there would be money he could tie onto."

"But how about the paper he brought with him when he showed up at my place?" objected Harvey. "It had all the boundary lines and the markers on it, and the location of the ranchhouse, and other things."

"All of which could easily have been gotten from the Land Office if Miles Pacer or one of his men showed up there as a prospective purchaser of the Booger F and desired information concerning the property that had previously been bought from the state," Slade explained. "I thought of contacting the Land Office to find out if somebody had been there showing an interest in the Booger F about a year back, but decided it really wasn't necessary."

Harvey nodded his understanding.

"The one weak link in his nice little chain was the danger of Dirk Pacer's remains being discovered and identified," Slade continued. "He evidently worried about that; beyond all reason, in fact, for the chance of such a happening was unlikely indeed; but, 'The guilty flee when no man pursueth.' That's why he was so anxious to kill Sancho, the only man living, so far as he could learn, who knew the exact location of the sand flat. Doubtless he also feared that Sancho told me about it, which might be the reason why he's been so anxious to do away with me. He did have Sancho's friend killed, not much doubt about that. Well, now with the discovery of Dirk Pacer's skeleton, and the unexpected bit of luck of the ring, I'm in a position to drop a loop on Mr. Miles Pacer for fraud, anyhow. So far there's nothing to really connect him with the Dawn Riders, of whom I'm convinced he's the brains, but maybe something will tie him up with that once the wheels start turning."

"I hope so," growled Harvey. "The infernal murdering sidewinder!"

Slade nodded. What he did not tell his companions was that he was convinced that Miles Pacer would never be taken without a fight, in the course of which he hoped suitable justice would be accomplished.

"I'll tell you the rest of it later," he told Harvey. "Let's dig a little more — I'm still curious about that notation on the old map. We've got to be getting out of this before long, though; the gas smell is very bad and breathing too much of that stuff will give you one whopper of a headache, to say nothing of the danger of striking a spark somehow and blowing us all sky high."

They went to work again. All three were coughing and experiencing some difficulty in breathing. Had the hole been less wide and long they would have been forced out by the noxious fumes seeping up through the sand. They had gone a couple of feet deeper when again there was the gleam of something white.

"More bones!" groaned Sancho. "If we depart not soon from this accurst charnal house, I fear ours will remain to swell the number."

A few more strokes of the spade and they unearthed the fragments of a second skeleton, much more disintegrated than those of Dirk Pacer's, a very small skeleton of delicate bones and a tiny skull.

Walt Slade gazed at the pathetic little heap, his eyes gentle, his stern mouth very tender.

"Strange how even the worst men can find something to love," he said to his companions. "This was the pirate captain's treasure. I suspected something of the sort when I read that peculiar notation on the old map. Perhaps it was his baby, and it died. He buried it here on the lonely flat. Buried it deep so the tide could not disturb it and marked the spot well, doubtless hoping to return some time and bear the little body to consecrated ground — and never did. Perhaps the map was stolen from him. Perhaps he died and somebody found it, and the story of hidden gold began."

Old Arn Harvey brushed his callused hand across his eyes. "Well, I reckon that's all," he said heavily. "I'll just take these poor little bones back with me and bury them in the churchyard with my folks, and Dirk Pacer's, too." He was turning toward the ladder when Slade stayed him.

"I want to dig a little deeper while there's still light," he said. "I don't think there's much farther to go, the way those fumes are getting stronger by the minute."

They went back to work and soon afterward the spades struck against an unyielding surface. Slade cleared away the loose sand and disclosed naked rock of a bluish hue. He examined it with the eye of a geologist.

"Fairly close-grained shale with the appearance of being somewhat shattered, thus allowing the fumes to seep through," he announced. "Yes, I'm positive that there's an oil pool under here, as well as a reservoir of natural gas. I presume this is all state land, eh, Harvey?"

"It is," old Arn nodded.

"Okay," Slade said. "We'll talk it over

tonight. Now let's be getting out of here, the air is bad."

At that moment an explosive snort sounded at the edge of the nearby thicket. Slade instantly recognized Shadow's warning that somebody was approaching. He slipped up the ladder and cautiously peered over the lip of the hole.

Stealing stealthily across the sands, gun in hand, was Miles Pacer with two more men crowding close behind him. Slade leaped back into the hole an instant before Pacer's gun cracked and lead kicked sand from the lip of the excavation. He seized Sancho's old Sharps buffalo gun from where it leaned against the side of the pit and raced up the ladder again. Shoving the rifle muzzle over the lip he pulled the trigger. The Sharps let go with a boom and a cloud of smoke. Startled yells answered the crashing report. Slade dropped the Sharps and whipped out his Colts. Back and forth the muzzles shifted, sweeping the unseen terrain with a storm of bullets. More yells followed, and the pad of running feet. Slade crouched on the rung of the ladder, listening intently, reloading as fast as he could. The sound of voices were more distant now, from about the edge of the thicket, he judged. Guns began banging at intervals, the bullets whining over the hole or kicking up spurts of sand from its lip.

"We're on a spot," he answered the babble of questions from his companions as he dropped back to the bottom of the hole. "It's Miles Pacer and what's left of his bunch. They must have tailed us here. I slipped, Harvey, when I forgot to caution you to slide Sancho out of town at night. And if we don't figure something mighty fast we'll all very likely pay for the mistake. I drove them back away from the hole, but when it gets dark the advantage will all be on their side. They'll slip up unseen and mow us down. They're keeping a close watch on the hole and sending along a little lead now and then as a hint we'd better stay under cover."

"What the devil we going to do?" Harvey asked as he drew and examined the gun.

"Die well," said Sancho, reloading the Sharps.

NINETEEN

Slade's mind was working at racing speed. He glanced up at the sky, which was already beginning to glow with sunset. Then he studied the side wall of the pit.

"I believe we've got a chance, if the dark

will just hold off long enough," he said. "I'm going to try and tunnel sideways through the sand and come up some distance from here. They'll be watching the hole and maybe I can get the drop on them before they catch on. Worth trying, anyhow, and I can't think of anything else."

"You can never do it, the sand will cave in and smother you," Harvey protested.

"Perhaps not," Slade returned, "the sand is damp and packed hard. With the roof of the tunnel arched, I believe it will hold. Sancho, you'll stay close behind me and pass the sand out as I dig. Harvey, you work back of Sancho, and try and keep a watch on the edge of the hole at the same time."

He took one of the spades and with a wrench of his powerful hands broke the handle across his knee, giving him a short tool to dig with. Then without an instant's delay he went to work on the side of the hole parallel to where he judged the outlaws were stationed.

With frenzied speed he shovelled away at the close packed sand, sloping the floor of the burrow gently upward, arching the roof to support the weight it was forced to bear. The sand fell in to some extent, hampering him, slowing his progress, but no serious cave-in occurred. Outside an occasional bullet whined overhead or spatted a shower of sand into the pit, warning the prisoners that the owlhoots were on the job.

Gasping, coughing, Slade toiled in the narrow burrow. His muscles ached, his clothes were soaked with sweat. The gas fumes irritated his throat and smarted his eyes. Sancho shuffled back and forth, shoving the loose sand to where Harvey could reach it and deposit it in the excavation.

Finally the burrow was about twenty feet long and the loosening sand warned Slade that he was nearing the surface. He dug a little more, then told Sancho to get out of the way and snuffled back to the main hole to rest a few minutes, for he was shaking with fatigue.

"I think they've built a fire up there, not far off," Harvey announced. "To give 'em more light to shoot by, I reckon, the infernal sidewinders!"

"It may give me a little more, too," Slade said. He glanced up at the sky, slipped his Ranger badge from its pocket and pinned it to his shirt.

"Might as well make it official," he announced. "Well, here goes. Hit for the outside as soon as the ball opens."

Re-entering the tunnel, he started digging again, slanting the floor steeply upward. The sand trickled down increasingly, choking and blinding him. The trickle became a rush as he neared the loose outer surface. He dropped the shovel, closed his eyes tightly, drew a deep breath and heaved his body upward with all his strength. The last thing he heard was old Arn's whispered warning, "Getting almighty dark outside."

For a moment the weight of sand resisted stubbornly. Then it gave and Slade shot from the burrow like a fox from its earth. He surged erect, his hands streaking to his guns.

The outlaws were squatted at the outer circle of firelight and less than a dozen yards distant, their eyes fixed on the edge of the pit. Slade drew his guns and took a step forward. His voice rang out, "In the name of the State of Texas! You are under arrest! Elevate! You're covered!"

The outlaws sprang erect. Miles Pacer turned to face the speaker. For once he wasn't smiling. His features were a mask of hate and fury. His gun jutted forward and the two shots sounded almost as one. Slade's left sleeve jerked as if a ghostly hand had twitched it. Miles Pacer fell back with a choking cry.

His companions were shooting as fast as they could pull trigger. Ducking, weaving,

222

Slade answered their fire. A bullet grazed his cheek. Another seared the flesh of his arm. One of the outlaws reeled, steadied himself, took deliberate aim.

At that instant old Sancho's Sharps boomed and the man's face seemed to vanish into a shredding of bloody flesh as the heavy slug from the buffalo gun tore off half his head. Harvey's Colt cracked and the third man went down to lie without sound or motion.

"One apiece!" whooped old Arn as he ran forward, gun ready for further action if necessary.

Slade strode to where Miles Pacer lay on the sands. Pacer was dying, blood frothing his pallid lips, his eyes beginning to fix. As Slade bent over him he whispered chokingly, "Blast you, what do you expect to get out of this?"

"Nothing, except the satisfaction of a job well done," Slade replied, touching the badge on his breast.

Miles Pacer stared at the famous star with glazing eyes. A ghost of his perpetual smile crossed his lips.

"A Ranger!" he breathed. "El Halcon a Ranger! Thought you were just another owl-hoot — trying — to — horn — in. Feel — better! Not so bad to be — be — done in

223

by — a — Texas — Ranger." His eyes closed wearily and he was dead.

Slade straightened up and began reloading his guns. "Well, I guess that finishes the Dawn Riders," he observed.

Old Arn gazed down sadly at the man he thought to be his friend. "I still can hardly believe it," he said. "He always seemed to be such a nice feller. Slade, how in the devil did you catch onto him?"

"It was one of those seemingly inconsequential things that trip up a smart man and scramble his nicely worked out schemes," he replied. "Miles Pacer didn't understand Spanish."

"Didn't understand Spanish?" old Arn repeated.

"That's right," Slade answered. "Remember the day in the Widow Maker when I was dancing with Teresa, the little Mexican dance floor girl? Well, just before you entered she came to the table where Pacer and I were sitting and asked us, in Spanish, if we'd care to dance. Just a simple question of a few simple words. Pacer didn't know what she was talking about, and he made a fatal slip. Didn't think quite fast enough. Instead of just shaking his head, which would have been interpreted by the girl and doubtless by myself as declining the invitation, he hesitated, looked at me questioningly. And when I, pretending not to understand, hazarded the guess that she wanted us to dance, he said, 'Yes, I guess that's it.' Indicating plainly that he did not understand what she said."

Slade paused to roll and light a cigarette, then resumed. "When Miles Pacer, as he called himself, came to you with his story, he told you he was born and brought up in Mexico. Is it conceivable that a man born and brought up in Mexico wouldn't understand the language of the country?"

"Of course not," conceded Harvey.

"Well," Slade continued, "right there I began to think seriously about Miles Pacer, for when a man pretends to be something he isn't, there is a reason, and most often one that won't bear close scrutiny. Incidentally, even before then I'd begun to wonder a little about him."

"Why?" Harvey asked.

"Because Audrey didn't trust him, and I've found that in such matters a woman's instincts are surprisingly accurate. Oh, she didn't say it in so many words, but the implication was plain enough. It impressed me and really introduced him to my serious notice."

"You're right about that," Harvey agreed

soberly. "Whenever I went against my wife's judgment in a business deal or where some scalawag was concerned, I always lived to regret it."

"Yes, I began to consider Pacer seriously after that incident in the Widow Maker," Slade repeated. "Although I still hadn't the slightest notion what was his game. Then I tried to analyze the reason why somebody was so persistently trying to kill Sancho. I deduced the answer was that somebody was extremely anxious that this sand flat should never be explored. Why? That was a poser. Next, who could possibly be interested? Another poser, for a while. Then I gradually narrowed down possibly interested persons to Miles Pacer. Logical reasoning, you'll admit. Pacer appeared to be the only person, of whom I could learn anything, who could possibly have a reason for not wanting the sand flat, the scene of the fatal fight between the man he claimed was his father and your two brothers, to be explored.

"I'd been ranging around in an endeavor to find somebody else who might fit into the picture, without success. I considered Steve Gore. There were some angles that made Gore interesting. He was the only man in the section, so far as I could ascertain, who worked Yaquis on his spread. And, singular coincidence, a Yaqui Indian rigged up a typical Yaqui trick and tried to kill me on the trail to Sanders, right after I had rescued Sancho from the Dawn Riders. But it didn't take me long to eliminate Gore; he just wouldn't fit into the picture. Which brought me back to Pacer."

Harvey and Sancho both nodded their understanding.

"I'd already convinced myself that Pacer was lying when he claimed to have been brought up in Mexico," Slade resumed. "The next logical conclusion was that he was lying when he claimed to be Dirk Pacer's son. Which would make him the person who wouldn't want anybody snooping around the sand flat down here. He knew very well that if they did, they'd very probably discover and identify Dirk Pacer's remains and that would be his finish. Incidentally, it was."

"Definitely," agreed Harvey.

"So I guess that takes care of everything except the 'buried treasure' down here," Slade concluded.

"You don't mean the baby's bones?" Harvey asked.

"No, I mean the natural gas and oil that undoubtedly underlies the flat, a continuation, I presume, of the big pools under the

Ray ranch. So I earnestly advise that you and Sancho take immediate steps to buy the land from the state and do a little drilling. Liable to be some real treasure under these sands, greater than any pirate captain ever dreamed of."

"We'll do it," declared Harvey, "and while we're at it we'll file three claims, one for each of us. You've sure earned your share."

But Walt Slade smilingly shook his head. "Got a few *pesos* laid away against an emergency," he replied. "Besides, a man in my line of work never has any use for much money — no time to spend it. No, it all belongs to you and Sancho. I'll drop around at your place for a free meal now and then."

"Nothing would suit me better than for you to stake a claim there and stay right on," Harvey answered.

"Perhaps, later," Slade conceded, smilingly. "Well, let's cook something to eat and get a little rest. Then we'll pack the carcasses back to town on their horses and turn them over to the sheriff. I'm not sure whether this section is in his county, but it doesn't matter. And after we get back to the spread I'll have to be riding to report to Captain Jim and see what next he's got lined up for me."

Three days later Audrey stood beside

Slade's stirrup as he gathered up the reins.

"And you're really coming back, Walt?" she asked softly.

"Yes, I am," he replied, and it was no idle promise. Although he was riding away to where danger, duty and new adventure waited, he was coming back to the Diamond H, and soon.